TERRA INFINITA MAP

The Dome-Worlds

CLAUDIO NOCELLI

Claudio Ángel Nocelli

Nocelli, Claudio Ángel
   Terra Infinita Map : The Dome-Worlds / Claudio Ángel Nocelli. - 1a ed - Ciudad Autónoma de Buenos Aires : Claudio Ángel Nocelli, 2024.
   250 p. ; 16 x 23 cm.

   ISBN 978-631-00-4378-4

   1. Ciencia Ficción. I. Título.
   CDD A863

WEBSITE:

https://nosconfunden.com.ar/

YOUTUBE:

*https://www.youtube.com/
@nosconfunden*

YOUTUBE SECUNDARIO:

*https://www.youtube.com/
@nosconfundieron*

INSTAGRAM:

*https://www.instagram.com/
nosconfunden/*

INSTAGRAM PERSONAL DEL AUTOR:

*https://www.instagram.com/
eddienosconfunden/*

CONTENTS

WHERE IT ALL BEGAN

Let's go through this path that will provide us with so much information that it will surely be, at times, very difficult to process. I will begin by making a brief summary so that you can better interpret everything that I will present here.

It is also important to clarify that the map that we will be analyzing in depth was obtained by the navigator W. Morris, who has crossed the feared and mysterious Ice Walls in the Antarctic zone with the help of Captain Butler (ancestral) and ending his extensive journey in the "Ancestral Lands" (which we will see later where exactly they are) has been able to obtain so much information to make another trip to the "Lands of She-Ki" or better known as "Anakim Lands".

This place, where giants, giant-humans and ancestors of ancient *Great Tartary* (The Empire that rose against the Custodial-Anunnaki dominion in our lands) coexist, obtaining there the great knowledge of the Dome-Worlds that surround our lands as well as the many civilizations and stories that we have never heard before.

That mysterious Giant-Human called "She-Ki" provided him with a large book with maps and all the basic information William needed to adapt a little more to all the new environment and beings that surrounded him for the first time.

She-Ki's book was a summary of the lands and stories that the ancestrals were collecting and that could help him to insert himself into a whole new world, William's awakening would be carried forward with small steps. Then when he was ready, he would go towards the path of the *Great Ancestral Library*, where a whole database was kept there, the stories of all the ancestral times and the knowledge of the Anakim poured in one place, simply something *magical* happening inside those cold gray walls.

Much later, the beings of Cassiopeia would approach the shores of the Ancestrals as if they were *"divine envoys"* to help with the contribution of their technology. Already without William, his daughter Helen, would propose a unique journey in conjunction with the Anakim giants and the Cassioppeians to carry out as many trips as possible to open the way to most of the Dome Worlds.

This would update both the Ancestral database and Cassiopeia, as well as gather information on advanced technology from other species and also include whoever wanted to join in cooperation with the final mission: **human freedom within the lands of origin**.

After a relatively short period of *"human time"* (to call it somehow) more than 200 journeys were made by ancestral ships with Cassiopeia technology to as many worlds as possible of the 178 existing within the Great Dome that we will analyze in the following chapters.

WHERE DO WE REALLY LIVE?

This question encompasses so much and is sometimes difficult to delve into, but we will focus on all the information we have obtained after all these years, which are not so many, but it seems that millennia have passed, and the answer we got does not fit at all to the official version of our world or our known environment.

The information I obtained came from Helen, a woman who claimed to have come from outside the *"Earth"*, so one might imagine that this is another story of an alleged extraterrestrial being from a distant planet, but this was not going to be the case because although we can consider Helen as an extraterrestrial being (coming from outside the Earth) it does not apply to the same case of the travels of other *"distant spheres"* that tell the stories about these UFOs that visit us.

Besides revealing that those **spheres seen in the skies seem to be part of a great simulation** of the colonizers as a use of another means of manipulation.

Helen's story was different from all the previous ones told, because she claimed to be human, and then how could it be possible for a human being to come from lands outside the "Known Lands" itself? Everything changed when she told me that across the known "Antarctica" other continents and

3

worlds existed behind, as well as other advanced civilizations.

As time went by, this story began to strengthen more and more, with direct contact and conversations, documents and maps that simply made us go deeper and deeper to piece together this puzzle.

The story told about her father William in my first book on "*The Navigator Who Crossed the Ice Walls*" brings us closer to this whole story of how so much information was obtained about the Ancestors, the Anakim giants and other civilizations that also helped bring this story to light.

Helen would then continue to tell her experience until today, that she has gone out in search of knowledge and to establish contact with all the existing (possible) races in this Great Dome, so that in the near future we can all unite against the Custodial-Anunnaki parasites.

I welcome you again to the TERRA-INFINITA, and we will place ourselves in the center, not only in the geographical center but in the center of all creation, because the human being was born precisely to fight against the colonizers that stain every world with their dark plans, as well as we were born to guard the secret and the sacred that is found within the "*Celestial Lands*", which is the source from where our souls come from and where we will go when we leave this physical plane.

In this book we will analyze the map that made us question everything we have known so far, it makes us reflect on our life, our past and everything that may come. Join me on this great journey that will be a before and after in the vision you have of the environment that surrounds us.

SHE-KI, THE GIANT-HUMAN

She-Ki was navigating the depths of the *"Norse Ocean"* near the "Dyatlov Portal", or at least that is believed from the last update received. It is worth clarifying that no contact with the Giant-Human has been registered since she has left these lands (at least there is no information that can be published).

I have not had direct contact with the famous She-Ki, but really everyone on the other side of the *First Ice Walls* speaks of her as a highly elevated being with incredible knowledge about the entire history of humanity and the civilizations that live out there.

I have not seen Helen again either but she continuously connects with the central communications base and according to her last report, she was in the safe lands of Cassioppiea carrying on a new plan of exploration to other distant lands.

Since the information was obtained that the Custodians had opened a passage through the Great Barrier-Membrane (Great Dome), speculations have been running rampant here. All kinds of theories and another way of seeing the worlds suddenly emerged.

Especially knowing that many Dome-Worlds had received

visits from beings from "Other Domes" beyond. But all this can still be very confusing, and for that reason, we will go step by step. Let's continue this great journey.

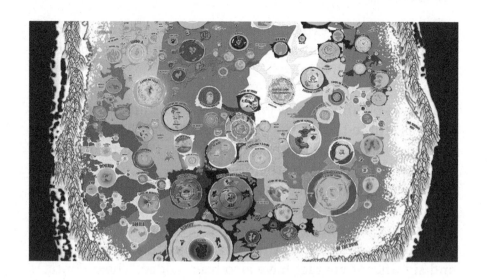

THE TERRA-
INFINITA MAP

The information that we will provide below is an exhaustive analysis of the complete *TERRA-INFINITA* Map, its passages, bridges, the 178 Worlds and the independent lands that are within the Great Dome.

It should be noted that much of this information is found in the Ancestral Database of the Great Ancestral Library in its Capital "The Ark" as well as the database of the Cassiopeians (Hiurenk) and all the updates of the extensive journey that Helen as ancestral leader is carrying out to most of the possible lands.

Additionally, updates from other lands and beings have also

contributed to the exploration and to connecting many stories and theories to reach a more accurate conclusion about the World where we live in.

Helen was planning a new journey but according to her report, she was still in the Cassiopeian lands, where the great base is located, which oversees the various plans to monitor each of the vessels departing to other worlds.
As of today, many journeys are being undertaken, with more than 75 vessels and respective ships, mostly equipped with Cassiopeian technology, although ships from other races that wanted to contribute to this great adventure of exploration and significant contact have also been added. These contacts open doors that had never been opened to humans and could signal the beginning of a new future in the battle against the colonizers for human freedom.

In the following chapters of this book, you will find the complete Map on different pages with its respective parts for better understanding. Now, we will go step by step to detail each world, starting from our lands of origin, and then reaching every corner of this mysterious Great Dome and its 178 Worlds.

WHERE DID THE INFORMATION ABOUT THE OTHER WORLDS COME FROM?

Helen contacted me a few years ago when I was investigating the possibility of lands existing beyond Antarctica. The topic of Antarctica and the many restrictions had always caught my attention, especially when one starts to notice that there are no commercial flights there and the establishment of numerous bases following, coincidentally, various military expeditions by many countries between 1900-1960.

The official and most important reasons for the lack of commercial flights, such as extreme conditions (the harsh climate) and limited infrastructure, always left me with serious doubts. Well, Helen's story about her father William, the stories that would follow about journeys to lands beyond the First Dome, the Terra-Infinita Map, and everything else about the Other Worlds around would be a cold splash of reality on our world, our past, and everything that happens in our surroundings.

The following ancient map, which shows lands surrounding the known continents, has always represented a challenge to the explanation of the current model. For this reason, the story that the Custodians, those colonizers who had penetrated the known continents a long time ago and carried out various manipulations, such as the climate, in these already existing lands, takes on a new meaning now.

The version of the Map of our known continents prior to past Resets would also come into our hands, and its representation is detailed in the following image:

MAP PRIOR TO THE LAST RESET (1728)

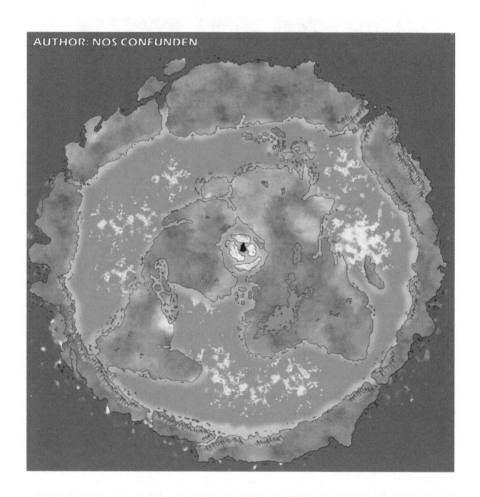

AUTHOR: NOS CONFUNDEN

Curiously, we found the southern part of America connected to the lands we know as "Antarctica." A new world emerged before us, leaving us stunned by such confirmation.

CURRENT MAP OF TERRA-

INFINITA, CENTRAL PART -
KNOWN LANDS - HYPERBOREA

In the central part, the information we received indicated that there was another unknown continent called "Hyperborea," which had been used by the first humans of Asgard through a connecting portal. It was formerly open to navigation, although it presents difficulties in reaching its lands.

In this way, we obtained a new map with the new vision of what Antarctica would really represent *a great dividing barrier* before the First Dome.

Now we can get an idea that our world with the surrounding lands, might look as follows:

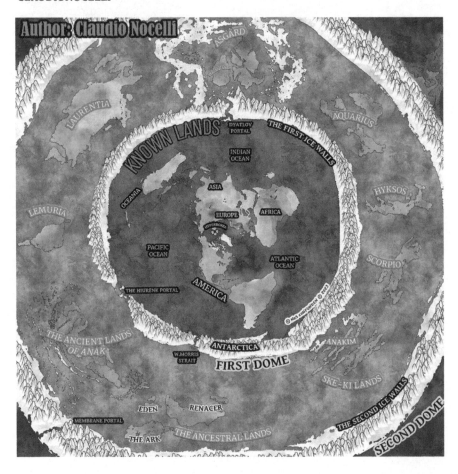

And then further on we will then see how our homelands, the worlds around us and everything about our environment look today.

The portals and passages that lead to the "outer lands", as well as the dividing Domes and their respective Ice Walls (artificial creation of the Custodians).

Helen continued to contact me, and several other journeys were initiated, with all the information arriving simultaneously. Time is different within each Dome-World as well as in the "*exterior*".

For this reason, sometimes too much information is obtained very quickly compared to the time that passes in our *walled lands*. My journey to Antarctica prior to all this contact had been key; the experience there and everything happening around us had come so quickly that there was no time to analyze it thoroughly.

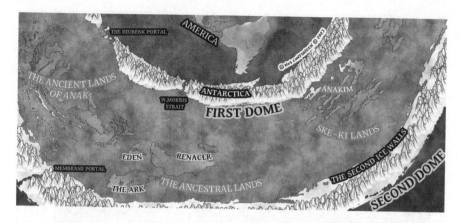

Captain Butler, the ancient one who had guided W. Morris across the First Ice Walls to the Ancestral Lands, is now on a unique journey with Helen to visit the many worlds around and establish a cordial and cooperative relationship with other beings.

We believe that in this way, it is possible to overcome the Custodial-Anunnaki power that seems to have reigned here for a long time.

The information you will find below is based on the database of the ancestral humans and Cassiopeians, with updates from both recently carried out due to the extensive and various journeys that are being undertaken and continue to this day under the leadership of Helen (ancestral) and Hiurenk (Cassiopeian).

THE DOME - SIMULATED STARS IN OTHER WORLDS

Before continuing along this thorny path, it is also important to stress about the different existing Dome-Worlds, as each of them have at least one dividing dome that serves as a barrier-membrane that also in turn functions as a means of separation from its environment to allow or block everything that exists on the outside from the inside and vice versa, of each of them. Following the point in my last book *"The Dome and Outer Space Projection: Year 1728 - The Last Reset"* we discussed the particular Dome existing within the Known Lands (Within the first Ice Walls) as it is possible that a great simulation carried out by the colonizers since the beginning of the new humanity (*after 1728 onwards*) in the skies generates confusion and modern theories that today little is questioned.

But interestingly, the curious thing is that in this exploration carried out by Helen, replicas of these skies have been seen (although with differentiation with respect to the constellations) which are also coincidentally under Custodial or Anunnaki control.

In this way, we can confirm that the Domes that project-simulate the skies we know today have been implemented recently in several Dome-Worlds, in addition to the Known Lands. Thus, we can find several "simulated stars" in the extraterrestrial skies of other worlds.

This is also an important step in the theory we previously presented about TERRA-INFINITA, the Dome theory, and the cellular theory as a structure of the universe of worlds that could be intrinsically connected and move towards the complex final systems that we are just beginning to understand today.

001 - EARTH - LANDS OF ORIGIN - KNOWN LANDS

CODE: ARB201

The **Known Continents** are just a tiny part of what represents the entire extension of, at least, the 178 Dome-Worlds that make up this Great Dome. And yet, many people have not even come to know the full extent of the real lands that exist out there.

To begin with, the First Ice Walls encompass all around in a circular form and somehow enclose everything within them (us). This is not due to any coincidence but was artificially created by modifying the climate and the environment to also cover what naturally encompasses the known "*First Dome*".

For a more detailed explanation about this particular "Projector Dome" or in general about the Domes that cover all the worlds, it is recommended to reread our previous book *"The Dome and the Outer Space Projection"* where it is specified and a better analysis is made about its relation with the membranes of the *known cells*.

In these walls, there are certain connections with the *"outside - exterior"* through passages or portals, in this case we have the known three passages (although a fourth passage was recently opened).

DYATLOV'S PORTAL

This passage has a direct connection to the Ural Mountains, which, through artificial portals created by the Anunnaki and Custodians that are now out of use, connect directly to the gates of Asgard.

The name of the place became famous in 1959 due to the fatal expedition of young hikers who ventured into this area. These portals were discontinued due to their instability in transporting matter, causing many inconveniences, physical and mental illnesses for those who attempted it, and irreparable damage to vital organs. It is quite common that when activated, they can cause severe internal injuries and unexplained burns, confusion, and sensory processing disorders, among other effects.

Today, they are well guarded by the colonizers and can sometimes be used for experimentation with humanity or other beings (although no recent activity has been reported in the Ural Mountains, and these areas are close to the centers of ancient Great Tartary, consequently, human exploration of these areas is not encouraged. The remnants that might still exist there are curiously found today under very harsh climates such as polar cold or desert areas that are difficult to access).

In the same area, there are several other portals, as well as in remote areas near major cities, such as the site of the "Tunguska Incident" in 1908. It is possible that the Anakim, during the era of Great Tartary, wanted to reclaim this portal for their benefit and to transport matter between the Domes, although it is unknown if such an advance was achieved.

THE MORRIS STRAIT

This passage is where the connection to the outside and the "gateway" to the First Dome is actually located. It could be called the only one, so far, that is really *natural* and for that reason the Custodians used it in the beginning as a way in and out through the narrow passage between the frozen Walls. It was also used by the Giants known as "Patagones" in ancient times.

The navigator Morris discovered it with his navigation thanks to the knowledge of Captain Butler, and it was there where he would cross to the ancestral lands to meet the lands and the great civilization on the other side.

HIURENK PORTAL

This portal was created by the Cassiopeian being called "Hiurenk" and was opened with advanced technology to help the ancestors to infiltrate the known continents.

The plan was carried out by Morris and Butler in conjunction with the Cassiopeians, thus many ancestors began to shower our Dome-World with messages about spirituality and connection to our source (Soul), stories about the true past and human importance as well as the possibility that other lands beyond the Ice Walls could exist beginning to question issues that had been accepted since the beginning of the new cycle in 1728 (Post last Reset).

Many ancestors then began to be persecuted, imprisoned

and much worse things suffered when the colonizers became aware of all this. The Hiurenk Gateway was also discovered and attacks were attempted against the lands behind the great Wall.

After their failed attempts were repelled by ancestral technology and the Anakim Giants, they would try again but using humans of the new cycle delivering their own technology.

The remembered "HighJump" expedition led by Rear Admiral R. Byrd, among thousands of other expeditions that began to take place. In conjunction with the creation of permanent bases in the areas closest to the passages and absolute monitoring. It was also carried out the implementation of custodial technology of detection of ancestral humans with radars that generate earthquakes in the area as an alert.

For this reason there have been several earthquakes in the Antarctic area as never before, therefore the Ancestral and Anakim stopped sending people as well as many remained inside the known continents. Eventually another way of entry would be sought and a fourth portal would be created.

BEHIND THE
FIRST DOME

LAURENTIA

In these lands we can still find Venusians, there are past human structures that were taken by the Venusians when the lands were completely empty in the transfer of humans by the Custodians to the known continents within the first walls.

These Venusian beings who are strategically located there carry out several studies and analyses and although we cannot confirm it, they would be helping the ancestral humans to be able to liberate humanity in the future or at least avoid another possible reset.

In addition, they know the danger that the Custodians and Anunnaki also want to attempt a reset in lands outside the *First Dome* that could seriously affect all the creatures there, for this reason in recent times they have destroyed several pyramids that were erected by the Anunnaki. *Recall that the pyramids are used to generate the great floods prior to the final reset.*

The Venusians there possess large laboratories and their studies are based on attack and defense technology that could help in a possible conflict, although the Custodians are aware of this and for this reason (and many others in the past) the relationship of the Custodians-Anunnaki and the Venusians is very tense.

At one time in the past it was theorized that early humans might have marched to these lands of Laurentia and built structures there, but this was later discarded.

AQUARIUS

Inhabited by hostile creatures possibly moved by the colonizers to complicate their navigation through. Several stories are found in our Great Library about confrontations with these creatures with sad endings since, they are creatures that have great physical power and can attack from the ocean itself, besides being able to create a parallel reality or "reality bubble" that generates confusion in the prey and ends up arriving out of desperation to the shores of Aquarius so that once there, it is easily attacked.

Anunnaki ships have been sighted prowling the area surely with intentions of creating new pyramids for future resets within the *Second Ice Walls*, for this reason the Anakim will promptly send personnel to check these areas.

HYKSOS

Lands similar to the above but which have been abandoned at present. No recorded visitation by advanced beings, the most up to date information from our database record reports that these lands are inhabited by possibly "native" creatures behaving in a hostile manner in Phase I (Initial) development with no major changes for some time. Which raises doubts about whether they may have been moved by colonizers.

In ancient times "Nibiran" beings (from the Lands of Nibiru) were sighted by radars and Anakim technology creating underground installations and bases there, although it is confirmed that there is no presence today.

SCORPIO

In these lands, there are different races of Giants, one of them known as the "Patagones" who settled a long time ago in the South of one of the known continents, "America". Today the area is known as "La Patagonia" in reference to these beings that were seen and visited many times during the different cycles of humanity.

There are two other races of giants that coexist without any inconvenience and unified some time ago to create a great race of Giants (different from the Anakim). The relationship with the Anakim is cordial but they are not involved in the creation of technology to liberate humanity nor are they prepared for a conflict against the Custodians.

According to the information received is that they did not agree with the creation of the Great Tartary since they knew that this could generate great conflicts with the colonizers on the other side of the Walls. In fact, today they are aware that the Anunnaki-Custodians could try to generate a reset outside the "Known Lands" and this puts them in a hurry since they will have to position themselves on one side of the conflict. Everything leads one to believe that they will eventually join the ranks of the Anakim in time.

SHE-KI LANDS - ANAKIM LANDS

The lands of She-Ki have great importance in all this story we are telling, especially regarding the map we are analyzing since the navigator W. Morris has received it directly from She-Ki, among other great stories that were kept hidden from the "new humanity" (the humanity that was born after the Last Reset in 1728) in these same lands.

In these beautiful lands also lies much of the ancestral power as the Anakim giants have helped with technology and knowledge over a long time, in turn helping to forge another empire outside the First Walls in the lands that are known as the "Ancestral Lands".

Most of the structures found here are of the "Dome" type and mostly white in color. There are routes that connect between the large cities that serve to transport large ships similar to very advanced trains, and these can be as large as to transport many people or cargo, as well as individuals.
They also have a system of navigation through advanced ships that take to the skies with great ease and speed to connect very distant points.

Their exploration also helped the ancestors to add information to the great database, knowledge about the past, other civilizations and lands behind the Second Ice Walls. They may have been one of the first beings to be able to cross the "Membrane-Gateway" from the inside to the outside exploration (although they have had great difficulties and tragedies in trying to do so in the past).

THE ANCESTRAL LANDS

Lands of great importance, here live the human survivors of the Last Reset inside the First Ice Walls - Dome and their future generations settled in these beautiful lands.

They possess various types of structures, although outside of the large cities, white domes predominate, as is the case in the Lands of She-Ki. Many survivors came to these lands from other Dome Worlds, for example from Mars or even as far away as Cassiopeia. W. Morris has arrived with his old ship to these lands where he was warmly welcomed by its large population.

They rely on attack and defense technology but have a strong connection to their past and the source (Soul), which they strengthen by dedicating a significant portion of their lifetime to developing and studying it.

Although their bodies and minds differ a little from those

of the new humanity (due to the modifications that the latter suffered during the *Reset* process) it is very complex to differentiate them at first glance. Regarding their interior, their way of thinking and acting is completely different.

They are extremely empathic beings and always seek the welfare of the community, they do not seek power or control the rest, although there are ranks, they always seek general consensus before performing an important action.

THE ANCIENT LANDS OF ANAK

These lands were taken over by the Ancestors and the Anakim after the escape of the last reset on the known continents.

Great missions departed from there as there are very important military bases, especially expedition missions to the Custodial lands (failed), especially in the ancient lands called Neo-Biz.

Formerly they were lands that were also used by the Anakim and other giant races long before the conflicts between mankind and the Custodial-Anunnaki colonizers. For that reason they later served as undergound base facilities, laboratories and a place of technological advancement for defense. Recently they have been visited by some vessels of possible "slaves" who have escaped and arrived there from the lands of Mars through the "Membrane-Portal".

LEMURIA

Lands that represent a great part of the lost human history of the past, since here were fought battles and rebellions of the first humans against the Custodial yoke. In fact, from there they began journeys to Asgard with the intention of being able to cross the great snowy mountain ranges and overcome the "Custodial Serpent" that the Custodians were said to have moved through these areas to prevent any human from reaching the gates of Asgard - Yggdrasil.

It is said that the giant-human She-Ki would have visited Lemuria and studied its connections and undergound paths before definitely traveling to Asgard (of this last trip we still have no information that we can expose).

Lemuria is an enchanted place for both the positive and the negative, it is a place of hope and a unique spiritual path as well as a place of past murders and wars.

ASGARD - YGGDRASIL

The lands where the beginning of human life took place, where the Five Masters gave physical life to humanity with their respective Source (Soul) brought from the "Celestial Lands".

They settled in the lands of Asgard because of the importance of these magical and dark lands at the same time, as well as because they were hidden from the rest and connected through a portal to the center of the known continents (Hyperborea).

These always well-guarded lands are full of mystery, so much so that it is said that some humans prior to the Resets were able to escape with the help of beings called "Archons" to the gates of this great land.

In Yggdrasil, its sister land, is the tree that connects to the Source of all life, believed to have a direct connection as a Portal to the Celestial Lands but which few have been able to visit. Although the Custodians always surround these lands, it is not known for sure if they have been able to stay there. After the conflict with the first humanity, it is said that the Custodians have also been expelled from there by an unknown force and have never been able to re-enter. However, they have brought colossal creatures to guard their gates so that no human could enter.

The creatures sighted there are huge serpentiform bodies with dragon heads, also titanic beings of stone that move erratically and Cyclops on the top of mountains.

BEHIND THE SECOND DOME - THE SECOND ICE WALLS

Crossing the "Portal-Membrane" we found 12 other little known continents. This portal required much study and technological advancement to be able to cross it and today the help of Cassiopeia's technology generated that it can be overcome more easily.

It is also known another portal to the north called "Bifröst" but this is not currently used by any known civilization within the lands already mentioned, it is very possible that it is used by the Custodians and Anunnaki, therefore, navigation or approaching those areas is avoided.

Also another area that we try to avoid even though it is closely guarded, is the area of the Atargatis Bridge where "The Path of the Giant Footprints" leads to. This bridge leads to the area we know as "The Abduction Zone" where there have already been several conflicts with the Anunnaki and other beings that began to abduct humans for experiments (especially at the time of the study of the *Celestial Lands* that I will later delve into).

The "Bridge of Hades" is important to cross the last barriers and finally go outside, what one encounters when leaving and crossing "The Path of Eternal Fire" are the free islands of Shangri-La (Helen together with her vessels have traveled this path to go outside to Cassiopeia and other Dome-Worlds).

ATOS

These lands are always used as a bridge to the Byrd Passage that leads to the Mars Dome World, therefore, there are many stories in reference to these important green lands.

There are permanent structures and bases there by the Anakim and Ancestrals, lately bases of the Cassiopeians were installed also with updated technology.
Today there is a large modern port with important radars and scans for fear of any intrusion coming from the experimental world mentioned above.

ARGOS

The area around Argos is always traveled with great caution because in the past it was taken over by the Anunnaki colonizers.
Although today, with current technology, these lands have been visited several times, and it has been confirmed that there are no enemy beings in the vicinity.

Curiously there is a small settlement of Giants that traveled from Scorpio with the help of the Anakim. It is said that thanks to this help, the giants that now live there send information by radars and scanning sensors at all times to ensure that travel through is safer.

TALOS

In these dark lands there were hostile creatures that had been moved by the Custodians, but with the installation of Giant bases in their neighboring lands and Cassiopeia technology, it was possible to advance and finally annihilate these creatures, therefore, navigation today is safe.

There are no permanent bases or civilizations living there, but there are temporary structures that serve as a control point for longer trips, especially if you want to leave or return through the Bridge of Hades.

AVALON

These lands are hostile and dangerous for humanity, they have great complexity due to their shape as well as the many bases installed by the Etamines of Draco and Grey beings of Orion.

For this reason, and although to date the presence of any leader there has not been confirmed, they try to avoid crossing this area, although there have already been several conflicts between Anakim and Ancestrals against the Etamines that still seem to be there.

ANAX

Here coexists a group of beings known as Orion Greys, they generally stay out of any conflict but, this race cannot be trusted because of their past and their direct connection to the colonizers and Etamins of Draco.

There are no past war conflicts in this area that we have in our database but certainly humanity does not usually go beyond the Bridge of Hades.

GIGES

Lands empty of any race or civilization at the moment. Many abandoned laboratories and other unknown bases are found there as vestiges of some race that has developed there a long time ago.

There was a time when the Anakim wanted to reach these lands to analyze in depth these places and also to be able to make an exhaustive undergound analysis, but the conflicts with the Etamines of the north made that this idea was soon forgotten.

Due to the scans carried out, it could be observed that there are several underground bases which are currently unknown. It is said that possibly beings from Nibiru could have lived there.

DEAD LAND

These lands are dark with large vegetation and mountains. They have creatures in Phase I of development although only reconnaissance and analysis of the surface was performed by flights through.

No bases of any race or developed beings that have lived in these lands were recognized.

THE INNER DOOR

These lands would be very similar to the previous ones (Dead Land) if it were not for the existence of a Gateway-Portal in one of the peaks of a great mountain that has caused great speculation due to the theories that began to be woven.

Technology has been sent there to study the area and apparently it would be a disused but natural Portal that has existed there since the beginning of time.

It is possible that it is a gateway to the interior and may have some connection to underground pathways to the North (possibly to the lands of Shasta).

SHASTA

This area since the Custodians took our lands and colonized the first humanity of Hyperborea-Asgard (connected by a Portal) was always heavily guarded by colossal creatures that they themselves were responsible for bringing from outside.

Between Shasta and Atlantis, as well as in Asgard. In this area titanic stone beings have been sighted walking back and forth as if guarding between Shasta and Atlantis.

ATLANTIS

From these lands we can also tell much of the history of the human past. They are one of the lands used by early humans in conjunction with Asgard-Hyperborea.

Vestiges of the human past of early mankind are still to be found and the technology there could be as advanced as some objects that were recovered from the time of Great Tartary.

The giant-humans and Anakim giants during Great Tartary began to devise a plan to be able to travel to these lands, but this was not possible because of the abrupt interception of the colonizers and finally the Great War.

Unfortunately it is possible that today this northern area across the Second Dome is heavily trafficked and used for Custodial-Anunnaki navigation, as well as by their allied Etamins and Greys.

MERMAID LANDS AND THE ISLAND OF THE DEATH

These lands are inhabited by creatures totally hostile to any being who attempts to cross or visit them.

There have already been several stories that I have published regarding Mermaids that confuse sailors and then attack them near their shores.

Red eyes at night are common to make these creatures visible, as well as other yellow creatures that exist in Island of the Dead.

In the great mountain range in the center of this island there are winged beings in Phase I of development that have also shown themselves to be hostile, in fact, there are records by scans made by the Anakim that many times they join together among creatures to attack by air and water any being they take as prey.

TERRA-INFINITA
MAP - DETAILS

TERRA-INFINITA, LAST
VERSION UPDATED AFTER
HELEN'S JOURNEY

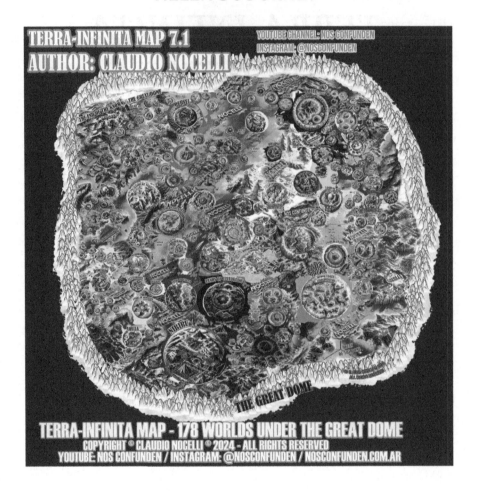

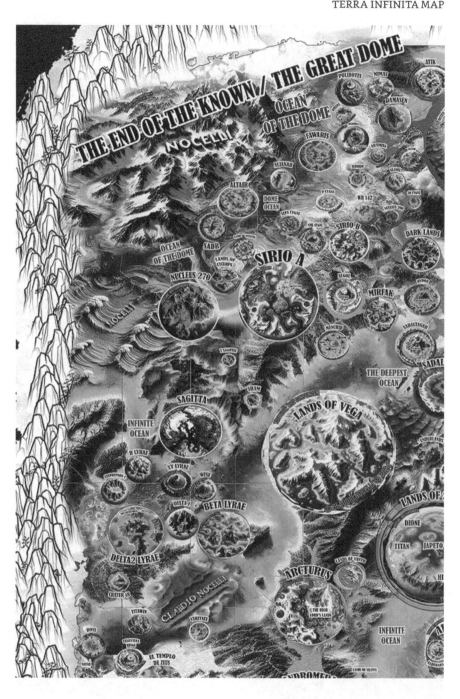

002 - THE LANDS OF MARS

CODE: ARB204

The Mars Lands, sometimes wrongly called "Red Lands" or "Red Planet", are lands of Custodial experimentation and technological advancement and of the Grey beings of Orion, although certain experiments are also often carried out by the Anunnaki leaders.

As we already exposed in previous books in these lands different experiments are carried out between different races, the most "punished" could be the human race that was moved there with false Custodial promises for betraying their own race. Thus generations are still suffering inside these great walls.

Thanks to the expedition of Captain Roald and other great ancestors who carried out several expeditions, in conjunction with ships that escape from there, we can ensure that in these beautiful lands of great vegetation can also live a great and dark hell.

It is said that in the past great celebrities from different fields have visited these lands and possibly settled there together with the first human groups. Life there is longer due to the time difference with the Known Lands.

We are not going to delve again into these lands as we devoted even a whole book, but because we added the Cassiopeia database we can add other areas that we had not previously detailed.

There are two distinct passages such as the Byrd Passage to the North and another recently discovered passage called the "Reptilian Passage" that leads directly to the Anunnaki Lands.

There are also connecting portals that transport matter, such as the famous "Gate P88".

In TERRA CIMMERIA great battles took place between Greys, Etamines and Humans in the past, the latter had to retreat and look for another area to develop, ending up in the south of AERIA to finally settle in what we prefer to call today as "Human Colony", although presumably they call it "Lands of the New Beginning".

South of the Human Colony we can find large tracts of land that bathe the Mare ERYTHRAEUM, in these lands there is a group of Saturnians and Taurians.For this reason and others, in these Dome Worlds there is great tension against the Custodians and Anunnaki in order to free them.

This information is relatively new as it was told by a human being who escaped in a boat with ten men through the Byrd Passage to the Ancestral Lands.

There are today great conflicts between Taurians and Greys, with humanity in the middle of all this internal warfare in these experimental lands.

003 - ANUNNAKI'S LANDS

CODE: ARB013

The lands of some of the most feared and advanced colonizers who have caused great conflicts and continue to make many beings suffer through wars, misery, and diseases due to their vile control.

As we have already exposed previously these beings have developed early under the Great Dome of the 178 Worlds and that gave way then to explore and colonize other lands in search of power and their thirst to be the most powerful beings of this Dome.

They are known for their pyramids to carry out the great reset, today in addition to helping the Custodians in exploration and conflicts outside the Great Dome also leaders who are still in their lands seek to carry out a future reset in the lands of the Second Ice Walls and extend their power in the colony called Earth.

They have also extended their lands northward into the independent lands called Endiku and Gilgamesh and have set up bases and laboratories there as well.

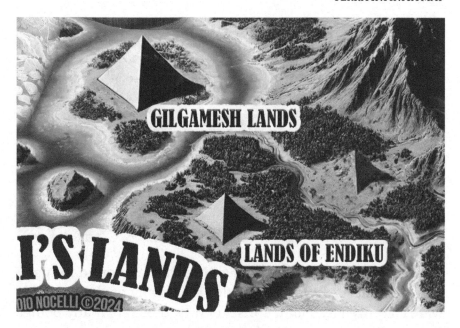

The central power lies in the lands of ERYTHRA THATASSA (BABILONIA) and its great base is located in SIPPAR, a crater that gives way to the interior where eight different underground floors administered and differentiated by laboratories and technology studies on other races would be found.

In *NIMROD* are the lands of the leader, who many follow and listen to in order to realize the next steps for the development of their species.

SUMER is also another center but here is another type of study that is unknown, although previously there were studies of the Celestial Lands (which they could never enter).

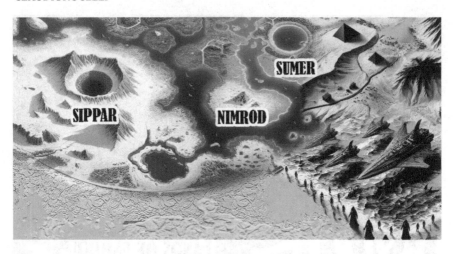

Their civilization is so extensive that they are found in many points of the 178 Worlds, besides that many of those worlds were colonized by them. Consequently, there are many beings that coexist in the great cities forged long ago and that possess great technology that is still unknown.

004 - THE LANDS OF CUSTODIANS

CODE: X001

Another of the most important lands due to their great manipulation and control of other Dome Worlds throughout the Great Dome. For a great period of time they were considered the most powerful beings in this Great Dome until the appearance of the Anunnaki and beings from Nibiru. To this World I have also dedicated an entire book, therefore, I will summarize much of this World and add updates.

It is known that the Custodians, or at least much of their strength, is outside the Great Dome by finding and forcing the creation of a passageway to the outside. Some theories tell that they regretted having done so as they encountered hostility from the other side at several points and now fear losing everything they have achieved so far.

This generates great uncertainty in all the other Dome Worlds since it is not known for sure what will happen when they return, for better or for worse. For this reason the Ancestrals together with the Cassiopeians took the opportunity to send many ships to the different worlds for exploration, since the most important beings (most of the Real-Leaders) are focused on this new conflict together with the Anunnaki leaders.

The last thing we were able to publish about these lands was about the exploration of Mik-ha, that hero who broke formation and headed directly to those latitudes under the darkness and fire of the Custodians.

Not finding any "matter connector" or Portal, he has not been able to enter and ended, unconfirmed, with the destruction of his ship and possible death.

The scanning achieved with the technology available at the time led to a better understanding of his Dome World, although over time we obtained more information about this mysterious place that is worth analyzing.

Its main area is the central core called "BAAL" which is surrounded by large walls and volcanic lava. In this great "rock" can be seen several craters from which also born portals into the interior (It is unknown what is found there).

There are several advanced laboratories with genetics of the different existing races, even races from outside this Great Dome have been recently added. The entrance-exit portals are unknown, it has not yet been possible to penetrate this area due to its great mystery and advanced technology.

The Custodians are known for carrying out colonizations of other races, squeezing their resources and eventually abandoning them, except in the case of humanity, who they do not want to abandon because they know their great spiritual potential and connection to the Celestial Lands could cause them greater harm in the future.

Regarding their morphology, custodial beings have the ability to change their forms into different species, they have done so throughout all the cycles of mankind also during wars. However, we can deduce that their form looks similar to the following:

005 - LANDS OF QUAOAR-X

CODE: N855

Quaoars are beings of small stature, insectoid, with a technological advancement in the range of A3 (**On the scale of A1 to A6**), therefore, they are in the middle of advancement in reference to the others. Although they have great spiritual advancement, even surpassing other very spiritual beings within this Great Dome.

They have with humanity a common enemy, the Custodians, who have colonized their lands long ago and after stealing their most important minerals have abandoned them many Suns ago.

For this reason the Quaoars could join in a possible future conflict of humanity against the parasites. Their technology based on attack and defense is not so advanced but they have a great technological progress coupled with spirituality that has surprised even the Cassiopieans.
The Ancestral-Cassiopeian ship SCB044 has visited their lands recently and has been received very cordially, their leader Anxa, has established direct communication with the Cassiopeians and all the information was immediately sent back to the home Dome-World.

On their way back we had a problem with the ship and the Quaoars came out of their Dome to assist them. This happened in the ocean called "Ocean of the Death" which is very complex to navigate because of the thick murky waters and also because there are guardian ships close to its great dark walls, anyway the Quaoar-x beings did not hesitate to send a support ship until they could get out of there to the north.

006 - PLEIADES

CODE: ARB004

Pleiadian beings were always quite reluctant to make contact with humanity (at least with those born in the last cycles) and neither agreed with the rise of the empire of Tartary, therefore, they always stayed away, but lately they are having big problems in their lands and are looking to expand or directly move to other worlds.

This forced them to contact the ancestrals who had no objection to help them to establish groups around other lands, they supported them with technology and creation of connecting highways to facilitate the transfer.

The disadvantage is that both the *Mermaid Lands* and the *Island of the Death* are full of hostile creatures and their navigation is complicated, and it is unthinkable for now to inhabit those continents.

Therefore, there is no possibility of entering through the mountain peaks towards the Second Dome, but the possibility of entering from the north through *"The Road of Never Rest"* could be attempted to head towards the lands of *Atlantis,* although first it is necessary to confirm that there are no colonizers there and that they can settle permanently.

It was temporarily decided that some groups would move to independent lands called *"LAND DER ERNÜCHTERUNG"* and lands further north in the mountains that are also inhabited by Pleiadians today.

The "reconciliation" of Ancestrals and Pleiadians can be an important starting point to create great bonds in the future, Pleiadians are great spiritually advanced beings and can help a lot in human liberation, as they did in the beginning when the first humans inhabited Asgard.

Regarding their lands of origin, in ALCYONE live great leaders, they seek the welfare of their entire community and major decisions are taken together with popular consultation. Most of its inhabitants and the most advanced cities are in TAYGETA.

007 - LANDS
OF URANUS

CODE: Y558

These lands are inhabited by their native *"Uranites"* and today they are in a serious situation, as some beings from other

Dome Worlds, due to possible genetic modifications made by the Custodial colonizers, are in danger of continuing to survive as a race.

The diseases that began to sprout in their bodies added to the strange climate that began to have their World are being lethal, such is the seriousness of the matter that new uranites are just being born.

Below, you can observe how their world was before the colonization, and then you will see an image of their world now with its manipulated climate.

They have a great vision and can observe several kilometers, their sight is really tuned, therefore, they are great explorers. They are giants and used to have a very long life span before the problem with their environment and genetics.

They are characterized by their gray skin (sometimes pinkish hue) and huge dark almond-shaped eyes, some of them have a modification in their eyes and are completely white (but they are rare).

Their technology has an A2 rank advancement, they do not have nor had great defense against the penetration of parasites in their environment, therefore, they have wreaked havoc in their World and were abandoned long ago. They are very spiritual beings and retain their empathy towards life in general.

According to contact with ship SCB089 the Cassiopeians and ancestrals had a great reception from their leaders and have requested help in order to save their race, a plan to assist them has been put in place and they are confident that they can help them from becoming extinct.

008 - LANDS OF NEPTUNE

CODE: Y556

Triton, Poseidon and Nereidon are its main lands. Here live the *Neptunians,* beings adapted to survive almost without any vegetation in a very arid environment and that today were able to bring forward by changing their environment to Poseidon flourish.

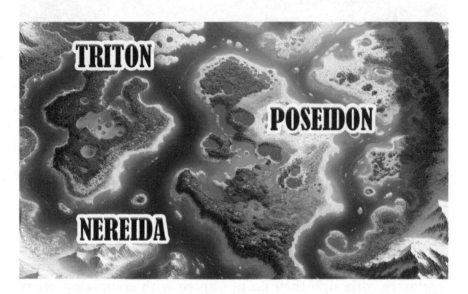

In Poseidon they built their great cities, in Triton live mostly their most important leaders, and in Nereida live very few people already due to the harsh climate that still embraces their environment.

 They are excellent at erecting large structures and towers, for that reason we can find many towers in their great cities and striking lights. They were colonized by the Anunnaki for a long time but were abandoned long ago.

Their morphology is based on their scaly and blue skin, their eyes are generally yellowish, they have a large tail that identifies them and helps in their fast movements.

Their technology is located in the A3 range on the scale. While they are not the best in defense and attack, they are great explorers, although they do not agree with colonizing other lands and always had problems with the Anunnaki.
The Cassiopeian and ancestral vessel SCB003 has visited these lands and the relationship is at a great starting point, as they agreed to help each other.

Their leader has made direct contact with Helen and they have also had deep conversations about the past, they are aware that the Giant-Human She-Ki is still on course for the gates of Asgard, the Neptunian leader has not seen this as a great idea.

009 - LANDS OF CLONES - SECOND EARTH

CODE: Y557

These are undoubtedly one of the strangest continents of all known Dome-Worlds. In these lands existed the most aberrant and mysterious experiments with many races, including of course, the human race.

Today it is practically abandoned, and everything was moved to the Mars Lands, where they have almost entirely exterminated the native Martians and taken over the lands.

America II, DNA, Organs Lands, Europa II, Great Lands of Deserters and Experiments Lands are some of the largest continents and still leave a large footprint for their abandoned structures found there. The Custodians and Anunnaki have established there a large experimentation base based on genetic modification of beings, then also used for machinery and exhaustive study on the "Celestial Lands".

The time here is very strange, we suppose that it is also due to experiments of simulation of realities, which causes very large jumps between the different days.

There are also remains of many forgotten and abandoned beings and equipment, matter transfer portals and other underground bases that we cannot specify.

The vessel SCB012 has visited these lands twice, without being able to visit all the continents (since it is one of the largest existing Dome-Worlds within the Great Dome), but we were able to make an important scan and study to add to our database.

010 - LEONIS

CODE: Y559

These sister islands are so vast that without advanced technology it could take several days to traverse them. The vessel SCB013 has visited them once, scanning their shores and the depths of their lands, finding no advanced beings on either island.

They have found creatures in Initial Development stage I that looked like reptiloids. The large vegetation makes exploration more difficult, but examples of the land and its environment have been obtained for future study.

011 - NIBIRU

CODE: X074

In these great and extensive lands live the "Nibirans", very physically strong beings with a great advancement.

Their rapid technological advancement and having found several Nibiran beings in many remote areas within the Great

Dome, make the ancestors reflect on several theories.

The Cassiopeians added confidential information about these beings, and it was previously believed that they might be some hybrid creation between Custodians and Anunnaki, but it was recently concluded that the Nibirans may have penetrated their Dome World and started exploring the Worlds long before the Custodians and Anunnaki.

This would create a big question mark regarding the spontaneous advance of the latter, therefore, it is possible that the Nibirans are behind all the plans and are actually the ones in control from the shadows.

We are now analyzing the theory that the Nibiran beings are in fact those beings that brought technology and genetic modification to the Custodian and Anunnaki beings so that their advancement has great leaps in time and they have been able to leave their worlds before the rest of the beings.

We do not have information about their leaders, we know that they could occupy the area called "Marduk" and that the beings use dark masks and are of humanoid morphology. According to some studies we can establish that they would be fish-humanoids, but it cannot be confirmed even today.

Their walls are impenetrable with the technology we have today, and it complicates the situation of being able to free humanity in case the Nibirans are behind all the technology used by the colonizers.

Their technology can be placed in the line of A5, therefore, it would be very high compared to the rest of the beings, some theories speak that they have reached the rank of A6.

They are also responsible for many of the races have become extinct, for their great wars and conflicts. The direct contact with humanity is also another question that we can not solve at the moment, we also keep information about it that is being studied to confirm it exactly.

012 - LANDS OF JUPITER

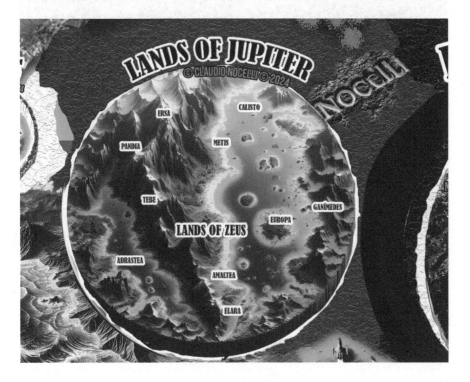

CODE: X003

The beings of Jupiter called *"Jovians"* are generally hostile towards other races, they even coexist with the Anunnaki leaders and are totally influenced by them.

One of our ships, the SCB007 approached their walls from the lands of *"Pegasus"*, but it was not well received, even almost generating a great conflict between the walls of the two Dome-Worlds.

Consequently, any future expeditions were cancelled and Jupiter was crossed off as a possible land for contact and mutual aid. In fact, it enters the list of mankind's enemies.
Lands of Zeus is located in the center and is a large mountain whose peaks reach considerable heights, even above its walls.

Ersa, Pandia, Tebe, Europa, Adrastea, Amalthea, Elara, Ganymede, Callisto and Metis are some of its most important lands.

Jovians are located in most of their lands and their population is well organized and distributed in each corresponding area.

There are large cities and according to our scans it has been possible to intuit that there are very tall towers that capture any intrusion of ships approaching their coasts. They are small in stature and are identified by blue horns on their heads. Their technology is very advanced and their range is located at A4.

They have really grown a lot over the past few years thanks to the Anunnaki who have delivered several weapons of destruction. The Jovians have also long engaged in genetic modification and experimentation with the human race from past resets.

They also tried to do the same with their neighbors on Pegasus and for that reason the situation between these two worlds is very tense.
They also had their great internal conflicts and for that reason many of them have died in past conflicts generated to divide them (based on the manipulation of the colonizers).

013 - PEGASUS

CODE: ARB210

These lands were visited by the SCB004 vessel of the ancestrals, until that moment it could not be confirmed that they were still alive.

Since they had a brutal colonization by the Custodians some time ago. The *"Lantians"* are characterized by their large metallic wings that they have created to be able to take to the skies and help in the exploration of their lands.

Their skulls are elongated and they have large dark eyes. In the *ILLECON* land lives their great leader "Kali-ba-nah", who controls everything from his position and who has told of his conflicts and wars against the Custodians in times past.

While the first visit of the ancestral vessel was well received and their leader was very open and friendly to answer questions and make contact, the following visits were not so well received and leave doubts about the contacts they may have secretly.

014 - LANDS HERCULES

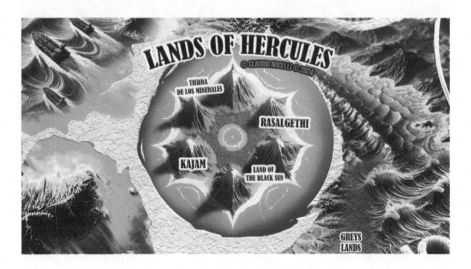

CODE: C412

The beings of Hercules are called *"Her"*, they were close to extinction because of the Custodial colonizers but today they grew quite a lot and even created colonies in the Dome-World of *Algenib.*

Lands of Minerals, Kajam, Rasalgeth, Land of the Black Sun and Argyre III, these are their main continents, these amphibian-humanoids settle in large groups being "Lands of the Black

Sun" their capital and where they forged and raised a great empire of strange structures that also go towards the underground part.

Their technological advance today is reaching A2, but their beings are very psychic and with a lot of physical strength.

The Ancestral-Cassiopeian vessel SCB005 has visited their lands and has been of great success because the underground areas were studied and the *Her* beings have taught how these structures have served them against attacks from outside in general for their development in this Matrix-Cell.

Another vessel would later visit them again (SCB015) to provide support in areas of need, therefore, we can say that the ties with the Her beings have been successfully established and, although their technology was not advanced, it also served as a nexus to assist the *"Angels"* beings who needed essential minerals to subsist.

015 - ALGENIB

CODE: C482

These lands were taken by the Her beings of Hercules, and their studies are focused on the area known as *"Lake of Immortality"* since they found in those waters important substances that could help in regenerations of their bodies.

Around it coexist creatures in Phase of development I (initial), but the Her beings have not wanted to harm them and neither have great conflicts been generated to share their lands.

Possibly the colonizers have not entered here or have left early without realizing the power of their waters in the core of these lands. The Ancestrals under Helen's command have begun an exploration of these areas in order to delve deeper into these "mysterious waters".

016 - LANDS
OF SATURN

CODE: ARB206

In this complex and strange Dome-World live the *"Saturnians"*, these beings have sizes ranging between 11 and 15 meters high (Titanic), and the structures found there are colossal, full of life and light.

The Anunnaki seem to have respected them, or so we thought, but with time and the visits made by the ancestral vessels we could realize that they could be under an eventual silent colonization.

Vegetation grows over these large tower buildings with unique technology and architecture.
Beautiful landscapes of fruit trees and abundant vegetation can be enjoyed in the *lands of Titan.*

In *Dione* there are colorful oceans, *Iapetus* shines with its large central island and the mountain range of Hyperion could leave any jaw-dropper in awe of the visual beauty that can be enjoyed there.

The large city that is located on the island of Iapetus comprise large structures and radar technology that serve as a warning of any intrusion of other beings.

They have large physiques and their heads are relatively small in comparison, highlighting their large jaws.
Their technology is on the scale of A4, therefore, they are really advanced in many aspects.

They have conquered the lands of Vanth in ancient times and now share them with the Arcturians and Andromedans.

They have provided great information on technology in exchange with the Ancestrals and Cassiopeians, and would be willing to assist humanity in their liberation.

According to the stories collected and the information in our database, it is quite possible that some bones from the Saturnians' past are found petrified in the soils of the Known Lands, as they would have attempted many resets back to defend humanity from the colonizers.

ARCTURUS AND VANTH

017 - ARCTURUS

CÓDIGO: C414

The Arcturians are beings of a great spiritual advancement, their leader **Vanth** carried forward a great development of the civilization in spite of all the problems with their environment.

Although their leader is not a great host since he does not like visitors from the outside, he has received in a great way the ancestrals and all the ships that we have sent there.

They are in a deep and continuous conflict with the Etamins of

Draco, in fact, several explosions have been generated during our visits, it is something that happens periodically. In the lands of *"Underlands"* there was a crude past war between them that ended very badly, as they were largely defeated against the Etamins' technology.

Also as a great gesture of help, they have saved the native beings of HOMAM from imminent extinction.
The Arcturians have elongated skulls and their clothing is generally red and flashy.

They delivered navigation technology to the ancestral vessels SCB001 and SCB003, and are used today for the exploration of other worlds. Their technology is located in the A3 line-range.

It is believed that the ancestral ships that were attacked by Etamine technology near the free islands of Cadmo existed as a product of this existing and recent link that exists between ancestral humans and Arcturians.

While they brought great help to the ancestrals for exploration and even for the entry of other Dome Worlds and other civilizations, they evidently need help against the war they are having long ago against the Etamins.

In the last contacts you have been informed that we need all forces to be able to focus on human liberation, and once there, we could see how to intervene against Draco's Etamins to weaken their power and avoid further deaths.

018 - VANTH

CÓDIGO: C412

In these lands coexist the Andromedans and the Arcturians (under the leadership of Vanth, as their name indicates). There are creatures in the early stages of development, but they have been kept away from the shores since they have been hostile at the beginning of the Arcturian conquest.

It has been visited by our vessel SCB003. In some hidden parts of these lands you can find abundant flora of many colors that make this experience a visual immersion worthy of the best paintings.

The Cassiopeians did not get along well with the Arcturians because of this conflict against the Etamins, although nowadays these conflicts have diminished, there is always tension between these beings.

The Cassiopeians do not agree with the treatment that the native beings of Vanth received when the Arcturians penetrated their Dome. Helen has put cold cloths to these matters making it clear that the end is greater than to go around with absurd conflicts for past issues. Vanth and Helen have a great relationship and carry out great exploration plans together.

Vanth - *leader of Arcturus and of the Dome-World named after him.*

019 - ANDROMEDA

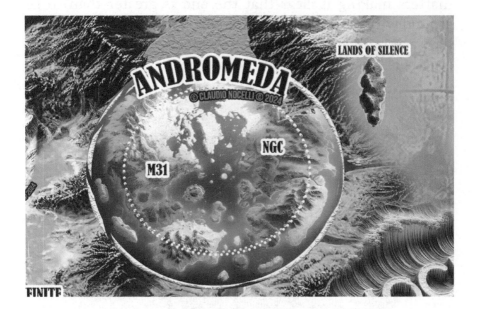

CODE: C413

The Andromedans had several contacts with humans in the past during several cycles. Their morphology is humanoid and they are quite similar to the beings of Arcturus, they can even be confused with the naked eye. They use suits with masks and some of them show their long hair of different shades.

Their advanced technology is in the A4 range, therefore, they have great advances in weapons created for defense and attack in conjunction with exploration.

They have carried spiritual messages to other races on Dome Worlds throughout the Great Dome, according to recent contacts with its inhabitants have confirmed that they were investigating long before the Custodians and Anunnaki about the Great Dome and possible passage through the great walls. Possible contact with earlier humanity, they helped the human JB lead revolt in Lemuria against the Custodians and escape the lands before the possible reset many cycles ago, attempting to reach the gates of Asgard with a craft but ultimately failing.

Helen visited the Andromeda lands at least once recently, and they have established meetings and made progress together for possible confrontations with the colonizer parasites.

They are studying in depth the theories about the Nibirans since the Andromedans trust that in them lies the key and all that is woven around the colonizers as the central mind or core to destroy.

In *M31* are one of the largest laboratories of all the known Dome-Worlds and research on almost all races is being carried out, from them we have also acquired new maps to complete ours and add them to the database.

In *NGC* you will find large cities connected by tunnels through mountains and seas. Their technology will be of great help for us to continue on this path in order to free humanity from parasitic hands.

While the conflicts of the Andromedans in the past are related to other beings (such as the Jovians or the Etamins) lately many ship-to-ship conflicts have been initiated against the Nibirans, as it is strongly believed that they are behind the whole colonizing plan. Even the Andromedans report that the pyramids were first created on Nibiru and then the Anunnaki adapted them to expand on other worlds to generate great floods and catastrophes around.

The Nibirans move with "red light technology", according to the information that could be obtained and studied, they are transported by this light that makes them able to move quickly from one point to another without ships.

020 - ALDEBARAN

CODE: ARB207

The so-called *"Taurinos"* have in their Dome-World two large well differentiated lands separated by internal walls and dome-dividers, *Aldebaran A and Aldebaran B*, but only the latter is used to live, since Aldebaran A was completely empty after a great internal war suffered by their beings because of the Custodial colonizers. In Aldebaran B we find large buildings and underground structures that connect the entire region.

These humanoid-taurus beings are really strong physically and advanced in their technological development, placing their rank in A4 (surpassing a level after the last contact and the technology that could be exchanged with them).

These beings also helped other races to subsist as well as recently helped the Angels beings to obtain minerals necessary to avoid extinction (through the ancestral humans as intermediaries).

Although the internal wars and the conflict with the Custodians was terrible for their development, today they seem to have recovered and to be stronger than before.

Their great walls are submerged by the dreaded "Infinite Ocean" which is one of the most complicated for their navigation due to its strong waves and changing weather. The beings of Aldebaran have been creating new vessels that can help them overcome this ocean with ease, but it has cost them many lives and lost ships.

They are in a great conflict that has triggered several battles against the Grays of Orion and Etamins of Draco because a group of their colony has been abducted and moved to the experimental lands of Mars. They are constantly on the move in order to free their brethren there.

021 - LANDS OF ORION

CODE: H005

Feared lands by many beings that live around them, as well as others who have had to go into exile due to their constant visits and abductions that they usually perform.

These beings are almost robotic in their actions and extremely psychic and possess a very advanced technology in genetics for which they usually carry out studies and modifications with many different races. Their technological development is located in the A5 range.

They usually abduct with the absolute permission of their Custodial and Anunnaki allies, they have large groups in different lands, as for example in the lands of Mars to continue with their analysis.

They have manipulated humanity in several periods and have also carried out studies with beings, they have also been in charge of the great human colony on Earth, but they have failed in the attempt to prevent the Great Tartary to rise because of its great technological advancement and strength. For that reason the relationship Greys-Custodians had not been entirely well, today they returned to work together as the Custodians are engaged in exploration outside the Great Dome.

Their most important lands are divided into *Meissa, Betelgeus, Bellatrix, Heika, Rigel and Saiph*, where their great underground cities and bases are located.

In *Mintaka, Alnilam and Alnitak* their leaders live together in large underground structures, which can be observed flying over the areas as they are open like craters towards the interior.

022 - LANDS
OF ANGELS

CODE: ARB208

These humanoid-winged beings are under great ice walls and large icebergs that prevent access and complicate the penetration of their Dome World.

Although today they are improving their situation, the reality is that they are beings with great diseases due to the pollution created by the Anunnaki in their environment and that places them in absolute danger of extinction.

They are differentiated among them by the colors of their big wings that come out from their backs, some are totally white and others are very dark. In their lands there are very modern and luminous cities and great structures that reach considerable heights.

The lands of *Uriel* are very particular and are united in all its points with its 7 points that end in large islands and beaches that bathe a cold and crystalline sea.
One of their leaders called **Azry** (with dark wings) is in charge of establishing direct communication with the ancestors every time we have visited them.

They have rectangular buildings but all culminate with red domes at the top. The ancestors acted as intermediaries to temporarily solve their problem with the neighboring lands of Aldebaran.

Their technological development is in the A2 range, but since many people are ill, they have not been able to make great advances.

023 - CASSIOPEIA

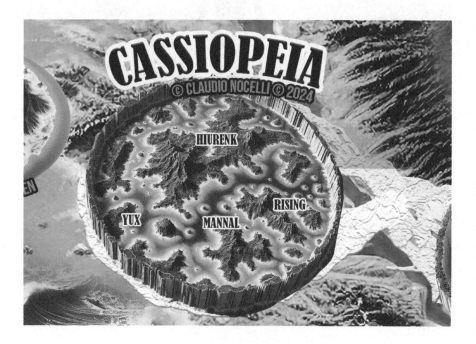

CODE: ARB032

The Cassiopeian beings have been helping the ancestral humans for some time now, their leader **Hiurenk** helped in the creation of a portal to go through the First Ice Walls and infiltrate into the lands of the new humanity, since the other passage known as "Morris" was not safe and was surrounded by military bases and earthquake generating radar technology.

Cassiopeian beings live in a peaceful way, are great explorers and also help other species around them. Large cities are found in both Hiurenk and Rising.

In *YUX* there are no beings and it is only inhabited by creatures in initial development phase.

Their technological advancement is in the A5 range, therefore, they are placed as great advanced beings within this Great Dome.

They are currently helping Helen (ancestral human) to reach the other Dome-Worlds, establish direct contact, obtain information and technology and generate links for help in liberating humanity from the Known Lands. Because of this great exploration they have lost several ships due to attacks and problems with the environment due to the remoteness of the lands they have been able to visit.

Their morphology is bluish humanoid, their eyes vary between yellow and very light green, with larger eyes.

Although they usually wear tight clothing and helmets that cover their faces.

Their ships have great technology to be able to avoid radars of the colonizing parasites. They have had great conflicts with the Custodians and Anunnaki in the past.

024 - CRATER 18

CODE: C4102

In ancient times the Custodians infiltrated this Dome World and took over the land annihilating all life there, for which reason the natives of Crater 18 became extinct long ago.

The Custodians abandoned their lands and were recently visited by two ancestral ships-cassiopeians SCB018 and SCB044.

The information that reached the central base is that there existed today beings in early developmental stage that are living on top of the great central mountain (*Mount Babel*).

Near its dividing dome there is a very particular reddish glow, parts of soil were taken for further analysis, no remains or structures of custodial beings or any other race have been found.

025 - BETA LYRAE

CODE: C416

The *"Betalyrean"* beings are very similar to human beings, according to ancient stories of the Cassiopeians reported that they were a human replica but without the soul or source connecting them.

Their functions are quasi-robotic and it is possible that any ship attempting to pass through their dividing wall could encounter resistance with automated attacks by a complex surveillance or radar system found there.

For that reason no ships have been sent to enter its Dome, but the area has been skirted to scan its depths. Obtaining details about their world, bases and place where their beings are located.

Their big cities are located in *"HET BEGIN"*, a mountainous area near the dividing wall, then they have underground bases in *"L2"* according to information they have a technological breakthrough there. Today we can say that they upgraded to A2 rank.

026 - DELTA 1

CODE: C4103

Extensive mountainous areas occupy this Dome World of Delta 1, the Custodians wiped out their native beings long ago and today there is hardly any life to be found in a primitive state.

The area can be used as a base for studies of the Great Dividing Membrane and the Cassiopeians are moving personnel to set up a radar base there. Leader Vanth of Arcturus is helping the Cassiopeians to settle there because of the proximity of their lands.

We have sent two ships there, SCB058 and SCB074, on their last connection they were entering through the Domo-Divider and will send reports on the depth of this world.

027 - DELTA2 LYRAE

CODE: N854

Very strange lands with areas of mountain ranges. There is a very difficult to understand place called *"The Sinister Sound"* where a sound comes from within the grounds, but the cause has not been definitively confirmed.

Although Cassiopeian beings have infiltrated inside the large tunnels existing there, it was not possible to get to the bottom yet as they are very extensive paths and seem to have been built by a very advanced race (possibly Nibirans).

The other lands are called *"Mountains of the Hermit"* and beings of initial development phase have been found.

028 - ROSS

CODE: C496

The lands of ROSS are located towards the edges of the dividing membrane, in the part of the nucleus it has two islands in which winged creatures in development stage II have been found.

Contact with these creatures was avoided as they were likely to initiate an attack or conflict.

Vessel SCB038 began a thorough analysis of the area and found forgotten Anunnaki bases in the southern part. Extreme care was taken as if Anunnaki beings existed, a major conflict could have been initiated in the area.

029 - CELESTIAL RINGS

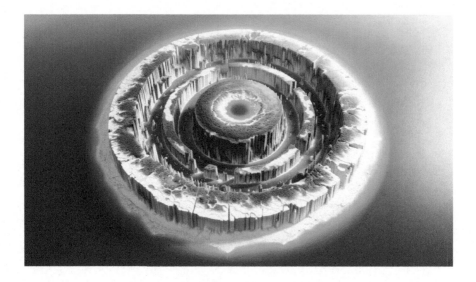

CODE: C495

The vessel SCB054 was able to penetrate and infiltrate these particular lands, in its center is the area called *"The Eye of God"* because its lakes have two colors and has a very great depth.

The Cassiopeians and Ancestors have not yet been able to initiate the descent to investigate the deep zone of the lake, besides that it carries a certain danger in case they could find underwater bases of colonizers or hostile races.

030 - MATAR

CODE: C497

Dome-World very close to the Great Barrier-Membranes, the creatures found there are not advanced according to the information sent by the ship SCB060.

Due to the harsh cold climate it is more complex to explore and for that reason it was decided for the moment not to initiate any transfer of personnel or temporary base there.

The part of its core seems to be like a great titanic tree that was cut in its past, it is still unknown if it is related to advanced past civilizations.

Besides being so close to the Great Dome could generate some conflict in the future with any race that may arrive from outside (even more considering that the Custodians have penetrated the Great Barrier-Membrane and caused conflicts with outside beings).

031 - SALM

CODE: C498

In *SALM* there are active Anunnaki bases and for this reason crossing their Dome divider was avoided.

The scans that were performed from outside by the same vessel SCB060 were enough to determine that their entry was very dangerous and would endanger the whole mission as well. It was not confirmed that there were leaders there, but it was not possible to enter anyway.

032 - TITAWIN

CODE: C4101

In these lands there are beings not very advanced (Phase III) but that could be in their last stage to begin the progress or development to be considered as moderately advanced beings.

These beings live in zones that we call *"CRES LANDS"*. Their morphology is fish-humanoid with gray colors but with different shades depending on the daylight.

The ship SCB065 entered these lands but the contact with the natives was not successful and they were attacked and repelled until the ancestral humans were able to leave unharmed.

033 - VERITATE

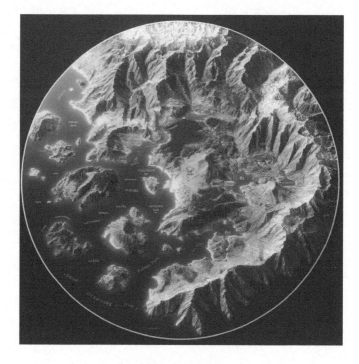

CODE: C4100

Little advanced reptilian beings live there, in the lands we call "PITA". These beings have morphology similar to snakes but with humanoid bodies, they are really particular creatures.

They are still in development phase II. The vessel SCB005 began the process of penetration of their Dome-World but red lights began to fly over the area and they were repelled by very accurate attacks (superior technological advance for their degree of development, possibly the colonizers are helping them).

The ship received impacts and had serious damages, the ship that flew over helped its crew members to get out of there unharmed, leaving the ship stranded for the moment in those internal waters.

034 - HOMAM

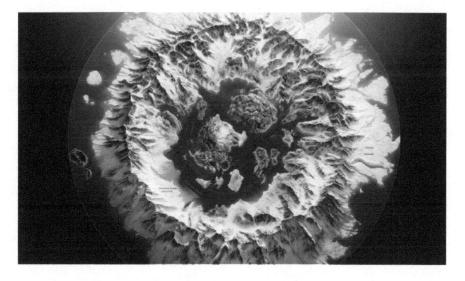

CODE: C493

The *"Homamite"* beings are in advanced development phase but their technology range is still in A1.

Some time ago they were very close to extinction and were rescued and saved by the Arcturian beings and their leader Vanth due to internal wars (possible custodial influence).

Their native beings are living and developing in *"SINK"*, their central lands. The leader Vanth (from Arcturus) has visited these lands together with cassiopeans ships that were sent there, the relationship with the natives is cordial and of mutual respect.

035 - BIHAM

CODE: C492

"Imperfect Lands" are the lands where the uprising of a small city of the natives is forged.

Although it was believed that these beings had become extinct, the *"Bihammites"* continued to survive and in spite of everything (including their harsh climate) they have made considerable progress in recent times.

However, this Dome-World has not yet been entered by any ancestral craft, Cassiopeian or Anakim Giants.

036 - TEMPLO DE ZEUS

CODE: C494

TICIO, RADAMANTIS, LINO, ENOPION and EUBEA are their largest lands and today they are mostly illuminated by their creatures in development stage III.

None of our ships have penetrated their Dome World but we have conducted analyses on the periphery and overflights thus obtaining basic information about their development and their lands.

No colonizer bases have been registered there, it is not known if they are hostile towards the other races, it was also agendized in the list to be able in the future to cross its dividing Dome.

037 - DIMIRIO

CODE: C490

In this huge Circle-Environment called "DIMIRIO" there are no advanced beings to be found, or at least, that is the update that was sent from the SCB014 vessel.

Helen has also visited these lands together with Roch, and they had serious problems with creatures that were then in early stages of their development (primitive), as these creatures attacked them as soon as they were sighted on their shores, Helen and Roch were able to get out of there alive.

In any case, we cannot yet confirm the underground life since their lands are very resistant to all the technology that has been used. For that reason, it remains to move personnel, install temporary bases and start with other Cassiopeian technology in order to obtain examples of the lands and to be able to penetrate them in order to scan them properly.

In *"Helvet-Z"* lands there are snow-capped mountain ranges that also have great resistance for excavation. It is possible that inside are bases of some other race, perhaps Etamins or races that are accustomed to deep excavations and sealing them with technology. Still the vessel SCB014 is there with 6 ancestral men and Cassiopeians as a plan is being devised for excavation with another type of technology that is being sent on another vessel.

038 - INFINITE LANDS

CODE: X091

These lands were once trodden by the natives but these were annihilated by the intrusion of the Custodians and modification of their environment completely.

Today the climate there is very varied and extreme, their lands are dark with no vegetation. Radar scans have been conducted from outside their lands as it is possible that there are Custodian bases inside.

It is not confirmed the existence of Custodial beings or of other races in its interior but in any case it was avoided to cross its Dome.

There is a portal P161 that its use is unknown as well as the destination location is unknown, it is still a mysterious area that was marked to be analyzed in the future.

039 - SCHEAT

CODE: C499

It is difficult to navigate and fly over the lands near SCHEAT, therefore, no vessels have yet been sent to cross the large DIMIRIO Lands.

It has thus not been possible to initiate scans or radar analysis. The updated information we obtained is that the natives have not advanced or made major changes with respect to their development since the last information in our databases. It is possible that the creatures there are still in the early developmental stage.

040 - CORVUS

CODE: C480

In the lands of Corvus, more precisely in Nebulae, which are swampy islands in its core, live strange creatures with colorful fur and illuminated red eyes.
They are of fish-humanoid morphology and very hostile to strange visitors.

Their lands are covered all around by very extensive and high mountains with some narrow passages leading to the Dividing Dome.

Vessel SCB007 and SCB016 have visited these lands but

attempted to destroy them, as they are not advanced and are in the early stages of development they have not caused much damage.

041 - AQUILA

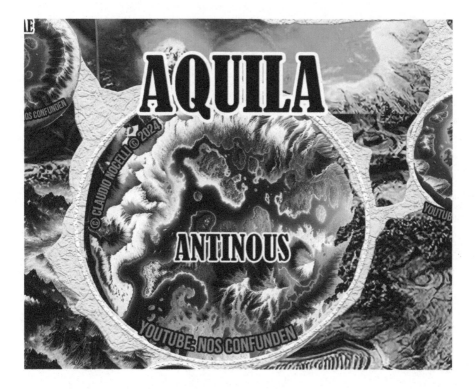

CODE: C478

The creatures of the lands of Aquila that live in *"Antinous"* that until recently were in an early stage of development have suddenly had great changes of advancement and development of their species, therefore, we can intuit that they are behind beings that are modifying their genetics so that they develop in this way, since generally the times are different in each Dome World but never as quickly as it is happening here.

It is true that as we said, each time in each Dome World is different as well as its environment, but we do not believe that in this Dome World there is such a radical change as to contemplate that theory.

Possibly the Nibirans or Anunnaki could be behind it with underground bases installed there with some future plan.
Vessel SCB012 has visited these lands and submerged in the deep waters, at the moment we have no news from this vessel to update with more information.
The creatures are of reptilian morphology and are found in the deepest part of the swamps of the central islands.

042 - SCUTUM

CODE: C479

The beings from Nibiru have annihilated the natives living on top of the great coal mountains there.

The ship SCB086 made maneuvers near its walls in conjunction with the ship that accompanied it by air, it has been reported to base on what was found there.

To this day no living beings are found there, only vestiges of base structures of advanced beings (possible Nibirans).

043 - ARA

CODE: X077

The lands of ARA are close to the great lands of AQUILA and also close to the great dividing walls of Nibiru.

Therefore, its navigation or overflying this area is highly complex, because there are many radars in the vicinity, enemy bases and it is really complicated to get there.

Anyway we have the information that there are no bases today of any colonizing race, their natives are in initial development phase.

It is possible that their natives have started again or that it is another different race that has started there with the help of the Nibirans, since the previous ones were possibly annihilated by them.

We cannot confirm that there are no simple intraterrestrial bases of the Nibiru beings, as it has not yet been possible to scan this area in its depth.

044 - PLANET-X

CODE: X081

The native beings here have become extinct due to the abrupt change of their climate during their early development.

The Nibiran beings have taken over these lands and established here as their "second world" and today have colonized every corner of these lands.

Removed from the list of Dome Worlds to be visited by the ancestrals for this reason, the Nibirans have no intention of making contact with mankind, since as we know, they are directly involved in the colonizations of the parasites.

045 - LANDS OF TYR

CODE: X070

In these lands live a very technologically advanced species and are characterized by their skins that are full of branches and vegetation, but their morphology is reptilian and they are beings of very tall statures.

Their rank based on technology is A4, very advanced. Their enemies are the Nibirans, with whom they had great conflicts and wars.

There are three different races within this world that differ widely but coexist in a harmonious peace. These beings are called *TYR* like their own lands, and their races are differentiated by *TYR 0, 1 and 2*.

They are beings that came to explore extensively their environment and surrounding worlds, had contact with ancestral humans and recently managed to establish direct contact with Vanth and Helen through the SCB052 vessel.

046 - IDUNA

CODE: X071

The *"Iduny"* are in an advanced stage of development but their range of technology is only in A1.

In the last contact with this Dome World, the existence of these aquatic beings could be confirmed, their structures are underwater although they also come to the surface to spend time during the daytime due to their skins.

Their fish-humanoid morphology makes these beings

particular, especially for the coloration of their scaly skin. Each creature creates a green circle where it dives as if it were a tunnel to its larger structures or bases.

047 - CALIGULA

CODE: X072

Here live fish-reptilian beings in the initial phase of development. It is believed that they were transferred from other worlds or that they are hybrid creations of the Nibirans

(Nibiru), since the native beings of the lands of Caligula became extinct due to the intrusion of colonizers.

These creatures have yellow or light green eyes and are very tall with scales on their skins, curiously they also create what are known as "green circles" which are tunnels to their underwater bases. (It is possible that the Nibirans also have a similar system in their lands).

048 - ADDU

CODE: X176

The *"Addus"* are humanoid beings of great technological advancement. Their technological development is located in the A3 range.

Their technology is based on attack and defense, and although they may appear visually as hostile beings and are surrounded by inhospitable lands, they are very calm beings who have received our ships in a cordial manner.

Their enemies are the Nibirans and for this reason they have established friendly relations with the Cassiopeians that could help us in the future.

Our vessel SCB017 has visited these lands among other inhospitable and very hostile worlds towards humanity, consequently, it was very risky to get there as there was no possibility of sending any rescue.
The Addus decided to cooperate together with the Ancestrals and Cassiopeians.

049 - BALDER

CODE: X068

The leaders of Nibiru have taken over these lands and their natives have either escaped or been annihilated in the attempt.

Today there are very large Nibiran bases and it is almost impossible to penetrate their lands, scans have been made from outside and flyovers, as well as other races around have given us information about these mysterious lands.

They are islands of beautiful beaches and vegetation despite being in the so-called *"Dark Zone"*, it is possible that the Nibirans have created underground and underwater bases, as well as have moved hybrids or beings from other parts of the Dome Worlds.

050 - HEIMDALL

CODE: X075

These are other mysterious lands in the Dark Zone that were taken over by beings from Nibiru.

Their name is based on the son of Odin in Norse mythology, it is believed that a species in the past could forge an empire there and its leader was *"Heimdal"* and according to ancestral stories were beings so advanced that came to the Known Lands to make contact with the first humans of Asgard.

It is possible that they were able to escape but it is unknown if they have established a colony in another world.

Although it could also be considered that they may have become extinct due to the forces of the Nibirans.

No ships were sent to this world as they are totally hostile lands to this day for Cassiopeians and ancestors. Their lands are very cold and mountainous climate.

051 - HEL

CODE: X069

These yellow-colored lands with large snow-capped mountains on their edges are inhabited by native beings who are in the early stages of development.

They have suffered several intrusions of the Nibirans and for that reason they have not been able to develop correctly.

The native beings have the reptiloid morphology with scales on their skins similar to those known in *Caligula*.

052 - GREEN STONES

CODE: X076

These curious lands of a very light green color that is due to a very particular vegetation that is only found here.

They were inhabited by beings who had also forged their empire in ancient times (according to the Cassiopeians). But today they are in the power of the Nibirans since they have colonized these lands and possibly annihilated every being there.

According to our radars we have been able to locate several portals (at least 3) that could be being reused with Nibiran technology, without being able to confirm it, they could be creations of the native beings that previously have been able to reach a great technological advance to then leave their lands in the exploration.

053 - LANDS OF
THE FINAL DOME

CODE: X073

These lands are particular in that they are very extensive and differ greatly from one region to another. We can find beautiful lush forests as well as erupting volcanoes annihilating all plant life around.

In the north we find frozen mountains and great walls that divide their Dome.

The native beings were colonized in their early development phase and for some reason the Nibirans have decided to "help" them in their development for possible future benefits.

As of today the native beings are developing rapidly due to technology that the Nibirans bring. Due to the impossibility of scanning the area we do not have much information about it.

054 - LANDS OF CRONOS

CODE: Y566

These lands are inhabited by very small beings that are in the initial development phase. Because they are coming out of the "*Dark Zone*" our vessel SCB017 was able to enter their lands through their Dome, but has had great problems to get out of there, since the time inside there is totally different from what we were used to.

It is normal that there is a temporal change in each Dome-World but in Cronos time has a notable difference (we could say that time passes *very quickly*).

Consequently, the beings there were in serious trouble to be able to return to the outside because their ship had failures as well as their objects became obsolete prematurely.

Their beings have a height of 0.40 and 0.45 centimeters, they live under rocks and mountains with ice, although no contact has been made because they are in the initial phase, our brothers have not been received in a hostile way.

055 - PAN

CODE: Y567

The creatures here are in the early stages of development, they are aquatic and can rarely be observed on the surface.

There are no living creatures to be found in their lands. There is a large mountain with craters on top of silicon. The vessel SCB019 was able to penetrate its world without difficulty.

056 - FOUNDER
LANDS

CODE: Y562

Lands of small extension where according to the database indicates that the beings of there were extinguished due to fierce internal wars, although the reasons are unknown.

Due to its distance from colonizing lands and the extension of its lands, it is believed that they were not colonized, although it cannot be confirmed.

Its lands lack vegetation and have a crystalline lake that is under analysis of one of our ships in search of life in its initial phase or minerals that could help in the future.

057 - TRANSMUTE

CODE: Y565

In the lands of Transmute there are beings in the initial development phase, however, previously there were at least three different generations of similar species that had advanced in their development and technology but were surprised by the colonizers (Custodians) and after intense internal battles they may have escaped or have become extinct.

Today there are curious insects that are being investigated in the laboratories of Cassiopeia that seem to be robotic, a possible custodial creation for possible research of exploration of worlds and manipulation (It was known this theory also found in other worlds about robotic insects created in laboratories).

058 - TITANIDES

CODE: Y560

 The Titanid beings were beings of great heights that were once one of the most advanced of the pre-colonization worlds and manipulated by the parasites.

The native beings of this world possibly migrated escaping from their own lands when they were attacked by the Anunnaki.
According to recent research it is possible that one of the races living in the Scorpio lands may be the ancient survivors of the

brutal Anunnaki attacks of the past.

Today live creatures in the early stages of development, lands of beautiful scenery and varied vegetation.

059 - DENÉBOLA

CODE: Y564

This world is just below LEONIS, the ship SCB013 also visited these lands later and found beings similar to those of its neighboring Dome World, reptilian beings in the early stages of development but with different pigmentation of their skins.

Other winged beings are also found deep in the forest where a crystalline lake is located.

Before going outside this Dome-World, a race that had not been encountered at the time of entry nor reported by any radar was found.

These beings are blue-skinned and humanoid-reptile morphology, by the latest reports could be placed these beings in the range of A1.

060 - TANIA AUSTRALIS

CODE: N8132

In the lands of Tania Australis there are little developed beings, most of them in the initial phase and some in phase II.
The most developed are arachnids of different colors and colossal size.

These creatures are found in the northern part surrounding a volcano that is submerged in ice and around frozen waters.

061 - EOLO

CODE: N8133

In these lands there is a giant volcano that is constantly erupting, the walls that surround it in the northern part are melting reaching the Dividing Dome.

The vessel SCB032 has visited and penetrated these lands. There is also an area of stone forest where it seems that the vegetation suddenly passed to another phase, possible past wars of native beings.

There are no advanced structures or at least they have not been found either on the surface or underground at a considerable distance that has been analyzed.

062 - LANDS
OF VENUS

CODE: ARB123

The Venusians are very advanced beings who have long continued to subsist despite the intrusion of various colonizers such as Custodians, Anunnaki, Etamins and Greys.

There is also a group of Venusians trapped on Mars, more precisely in Hellas Planitia and for that reason the conflict escalated to another level against the colonizing parasites.

The leaders of Venus are very respected in the other worlds, and for that reason in the past when the Custodians penetrated their lands they reached an agreement where they requested the liberation of humanity, although this was not accepted.

It is said that the first humans and the Venusians have helped each other and that some escaped to their lands through the north of Asgard by means of portals.

When the Custodians chased the first humans through several of the lands near the first and second Dome during the first battle. Today they are in contact with Helen and the Ancestrals, they are also searching for She-Ki around the lands of Asgard, for security reasons we can not expose more information about these contacts.

RUTH, MEITNER, GREGORY, CUNITZ e ISABELLA are the most important lands and where the Venusians carried out great fortifications, temples and very advanced cities.
Their technological development is in the A4 range.

They have bluish skin and very long white hair. Attempts were made to send several ships to these lands of Venus that are still arriving, the problem is that they are in a complex place due to the Etamines and Orion radars in the surrounding areas.

SCB002 and SCB083 are on their way and the Venusian leaders are aware.

063 - CELESTIAL LANDS - TERRA INCOGNITA

CODE: K001

The most mysterious lands of all 178 Worlds of this Great Dome and quite possibly of other Domes as well, since here is kept the nexus with the human creation and the connection with the souls (the source). Humanity was created by the Five Masters to fight against the colonizers and thus prevent them from entering these lands, the greatest secret is kept and possibly the direct connection also with the Dome of the "Forgotten Gods".

The colonizers tried with all their strength and technology to enter there but have failed miserably, other beings have also been used but the missions have failed, every physical being that crosses its dividing Dome ends up disintegrating completely seconds later.
With human beings they have discovered that when they discarnate physically they connect directly with these lands through their "Source" or better known as Soul that returns to these lands.

For this reason the human colony has not been abandoned by the colonizing parasites as they have done in other worlds, and the fight for these lands is considered essential.

064 - LACERTA'S LANDS

CODE: N8125

On this Dome-World live the "*Lacertians*" but they are usually not seen on the surface but in modern underground structures they have built long ago.

They gather in the *"Lands of Shesha"* and in their large laboratories with the research they carry out. They are of reptilian morphology, spiritual beings and technological advancement in the A4 range.

They have great weapons of destruction for attack and their structures under the lands are adapted for any attack coming from outside. Our vessel SCB034 has visited these lands successfully but has had to retreat due to being driven out of there.

It is confirmed that while they are in great conflict with the Anunnaki they do not want to engage with humans. Many of the native beings have expanded their lands into the nearby independent lands called *"Reptile Land"*, where they created large intraterrestrial cities under a large mountain.

065 - ARCANE ISLAND

CODE: C487

In these lands lived some giant beings who knew how to leave their Dome World and explore other worlds in remote times, even reached the Known Lands and managed to help some of the Second Generation of humanity to escape during the beginning of the Reset (this was done by the leader called *Hulex*).

It is unknown where this race is located as it has completely disappeared.

Today there are winged creatures in their lands in the early stages of development, no contact has been made and our ships have not visited these ancient lands yet.

066 - LANDS OF DRACO

CODE: N853

World of the "ETAMINES" those very advanced beings that are helping the Custodians and Anunnaki to colonize other lands and modify their genetics. They are manipulative beings and often control other worlds based on strategies to generate internal wars and then weaken the entire race there to appropriate their minerals or their entire world.

Their power and technological development is located in the advanced range of A4, they possess great weapons based on free energy that can completely damage small Worlds.

They are considered brothers of the Orion Greys and usually together they are also in charge of abductions to other races. They also play a very important role on the experimental world of Mars.

Their morphology is varied but their leaders are green Insectoids and are characterized by their large black or green eyes (resembling a praying Mantis).

067 - PERSEI

CODE: N846

The *"Perseinites"* are the natives of these immense lands that wanted to be conquered several times in the past. Great battles were fought against the Custodians and Anunnaki in these beautiful lands and their shores were bathed in native blood.

The beings here are giants and their skins look like stone, therefore, their movements are heavy and slow but they have great technological advancement that has helped them to move from one place to another quickly. Their technological development is in the A3 range.

They have explored other worlds in ancient times but they do not agree to colonize other lands but on the contrary, they are in favor of the liberation of all lands including Earth from humans.
The ancestrals made contact with them and exchanged technology during the visit of the ship SCB014.

Their lands are well differentiated in two internal Domes and are thus divided into *INNER and OUTER Worlds*, their beings live in the core part, more precisely near the great mountain that has a huge crater in the central part.

068 - SIRIO A

CODE: C425

The beings of Sirius A are called "Sirius" and live in the great city of *SOTIS*. These beings have had great battles against their brothers in Sirius B, in fact, these wars were so cruel that their brothers have been annihilated and today only these lands are active.

There were doubts about the visit to these lands because it had not been possible to confirm their benevolence towards humans, but the ship SCB012 has visited their lands and they were well received by their natives.

The beings of there are very white complexion and long white hair, their technology is today in the A4 range and they have very fast ships to be able to go from one point to another by air. Their ships on the other hand do not have similar characteristics and are quite backward, therefore, the ancestors have exchanged technology with them.

069 - SIRIO B

CODE: N828

The beings of Sirius B were sadly annihilated by their brothers of Sirius A by very extensive internal wars where weapons of mass destruction were used due to the advanced technology that has annihilated all life in these lands.

Today there is life in *AURIGAE* that rose practically from the ashes and little vegetation began to flourish again timidly due to its great environment that controls this Dome-World as a way to regenerate. But they are still in the initial development phase.

070 - VEGA

CODE: C419

On this Dome World live the native *"Vegans"* who have been colonized by the Anunnaki and have completely changed their destiny. These beings were born with another purpose but today they are totally dominated by the colonizers.

So much so that even their technology is based on weapons of destruction and they help the Anunnaki to create pyramids to generate resets in other lands as well as in battles outside their Circle-Environment or Matrix-Cell.

Their current technology ranges from A3 to A4. Their leader with the same name as their lands lives apart in the core part of their lands. It has been decided not to send ancestral vessels.

The Vegans in conjunction with the Anunnaki carried out the colonization of the SADALMELIK lands.

071 - SHAM

CODE: C418

Here live the *"Shammites"* who were in an initial developmental phase but today advanced rapidly to become beings of A1 technological advancement. This abrupt change could be due to Anunnaki manipulation that may also be influencing these beings to modify their destiny and end up benefiting from them in the future.

The shammites are insectoid beings of different colors, but generally dark green in color and very large red eyes. No ancestral craft have been sent.

072 - SAGITTA

CODE: C417

This Dome-World is of the *"Saggitans"*, insectoids of short stature and gray skins with huge green and light blue eyes.

They were colonized long ago by the Custodians and are believed to still influence these lands closely.

In their core under thick layers of ice according to scans with our radars made from the vessel SCB001, we managed to establish a possible Custodial mobile base that is close to the core of these lands.

Its technology is in the A3 range due to the fact that the Custodians brought more technology in recent times to generate a considerable jump.

These lands are being studied since this custodian base could be of great help in case of being able to infiltrate there, although no plan to carry it out has been initiated yet, if it is possible to confirm that this base is empty, it could be attempted to infiltrate in search of forgotten technology.

073 - SADALMELIK

CODE: N820

These lands were colonized by the Anunnaki and the Vegans long ago, consequently, their native beings *"Meliks"* promptly rebelled and managed to free themselves (as the Anunnaki were not interested in their lands and the power of the Vegans failed to stop them).

Since then these insectoids are totally against colonization and are enemies of the Vegans and Anunnaki beings. Their current technology is in the A2 range, and although they are not highly developed, their craft are too advanced for their rank.

The Ancestors with the SCB101 craft were able to penetrate their Divider Dome and establish direct contact with them. Although there was no leader, it was possible to obtain information since they provided support and support to be able to withdraw avoiding the waters of Draco.

074 - SADALTAGER

CODE: N821

The *"Tagers"* were colonized by the Custodians and forgotten with time, their lands were left free and they took advantage of this to resurge from their near extinction.

Their land called *"NARADA"* is a great mountain that reaches impressive heights and its climate changes as one ascends.

Their morphology is insectoid, and their colors vary according to their type. Their technology is developed in the A2 range as of today.
They have had great internal wars in their past due to Custodial manipulation.

The ancestral vessel SCB103 has visited these lands but has not achieved contact since their leader did not want to receive them and their inhabitants did not try to attack but did not show benevolence either.

075 - ALFA CYGNI

CODE: N829

The native beings of Alpha Cygni who are referred to as "Alpha" are very advanced highly psychic beings.

Their technology is stuck in the A2 range as they were colonized in the past by the Anunnaki.
There are still to this day several pyramids that were built by the colonizers in the past to control them.

Today it is believed that they are free as they were abandoned long ago, however we cannot confirm this as no ships have been sent there.

076 - NML CYGNI

CODE: N830

The natives of *NML CYGNI* are the brothers of the Alpha beings, they are also great psychic beings with the same technological advancement of the A2 rank, although the "Nemels" have managed to go outside their Dome World and have established contact with the Vegans, for this reason it was avoided to send ships since it is very possible their contact with the Anunnaki.

ARMAROS is their central land and is where they have their great core-base.

No vessels have been sent to this world.

077 - CYCLOPS

CODE: N833

The *"Cyclops"* beings coexist here with another race that also seem to be native, curiously it is one of the few Dome-Worlds where there are two races advancing at the same time that are considered native to a region or World.

Although according to the experience of the Cassiopeians they consider that this is due to possible genetic manipulations of some colonizer (Greys or Etamines).

They have only one frontal eye and are gigantic beings (between 2.50 and 3 meters high).

No boat has been sent to make contact with the Cyclops but the situation is being analyzed to be able to do it in the future.

Their lands are divided in *MYCENAE and TIRYNS* but in the north of their World it is empty of advanced beings (insects in initial development were found).

078 - SADR

CODE: N832

This Dome-World is really difficult to understand (except for a manipulation of the parasites) as we find beings very similar to the Cyclops but they seem to act erratically according to our radars and research from other lands.

These "brothers" of the Cyclopes seem to be hostile to outside races and are very closed in their community. Possibly genetically manipulated by past conquerors. They live in the central lands called *"ROM"* and do not cross water or have advanced ships.

Their stature changes considerably from one being to another, there are giant beings up to 4 meters tall and others simply do not reach 1.60 meters.

079 - EFIALTES

CODE: N836

In these lands live beings of arachnid morphology of very large dimensions. Their development is in Initial Phase I.

Our ships have not yet reached this world to perform exhaustive analysis. So far, our scanners have not detected any large advanced structures or traces of races that have colonized in the past.

080 - ALTAIR

CODE: N827

In these lands are found beings in initial development phase I. Morphology: Reptilians. No ships have been sent so far that have entered this Dome-World.

Its lands are divided into *X1Z and X2Z*, although the eastern part of this world has not been scanned with our technology, the reason is unknown and it is possible that it has some layer of security imposed by some advanced race. Vessels will be sent soon to investigate closely.

081 - ALJANAH

CODE: N835

In these lands live beings that have recently surpassed their Initial Phase to place themselves in the A1 range of technological development. Their morphology is amphibious and they can be found in various environments of their own environment.

While their structures are very basic they were still benevolent to the SCB038 vessel we sent from Cassiopeia.

They have reported no leader or pyramidal hierarchy, we believe this species recently started their group and was not manipulated by any colonizing race from outside. Their main land is called *AMMONIUS*, and there is a large base of these native beings as well as underground structures, their beings we call *"Ammons"*.

082 - FAWARIS

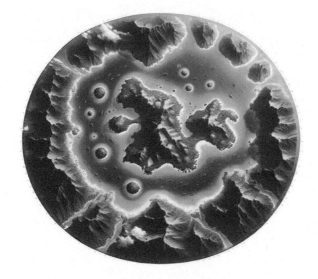

CODE: N834

The lands surrounding the Great *Dome Ocean*, its central lands are called *RYMNH* and there coexist two very different species that have already had several internal conflicts but today seem to live together in peace since the Custodians left their lands some time ago.

It is possible that one of the races that live there were brought from outside by the colonizers and for that reason they were forced to share these lands.

The most advanced race found there are beings of reptilian

morphology similar to snakes with greenish-yellow scaly skin.

Our vessel SCB056 has visited these lands.

083 - P CYGNI

CODE: N831

Lands that cannot be visited due to their high toxicity within their environment, for some reason after their native beings have become extinct they did not re-establish themselves as usually happens on other Dome-Worlds (other Worlds have been discovered recently that suffer from the same problem).

Therefore, no ships have been sent to penetrate the Dome Divider but have been scanned and analyzed from the outside.

084 - MIRFAK

CODE: C422

VIMARA and KUMARA are the main lands of this Dome World called Mirfak.

The lands of *VIMARA* are full of beings in the early stages of development but their sizes are colossal and their arachnid morphology even generates some fear for their possible hostility and venom.

We have not entered with any vessel but the vessel SCB059

traveled through the area of several worlds until it reached the extensive Dome-World of SADALSUUD.

085 - ALGOL

CODE: C423

In this central island called DÄMON there are beings similar to those found in MIRFAK but more advanced than the previous ones.

They are hostile to other races coming from outside and have annihilated other living beings around their lands. No information could be obtained about their seas, possibly there is no life there or it is at a great depth.

It is also not confirmed that there is any advanced structure of other colonizing races or that there are traces of previous life. Our vessel SCB059 has also carried out studies and analysis from outside its world.

086 - MENCHIB

CODE: C424

Beings in initial development stage II. Their technology was not yet developed to be considered advanced or to make any contact.

Being close to ALGOL and MIRFAK and meeting in a similar way, it was theorized that some advanced colonizing race may have impeded and interrupted their progress to restart these worlds with hybrid creatures.

Here we find beings of serpentiform morphology that are found living underneath the so-called *DOME-C* Central Dome. Similar beings are also found coexisting in the remaining Domes *Dome-Y and Dome-X* beneath large snow-capped mountains.

In any case, the structure of Dome-C seems to be an artificial construction of some advanced race, therefore, this theory can go hand in hand with the one that relates these creatures with genetic modification of possible Etamins or Orion Greys.

087 - WR142

CODE: N837

The beings living in this Dome World are reptilian but have undergone great changes in their bodies. Nowadays they are in advanced development phase A1, therefore, we tried to make contact through our vessel SCB005, but the mission was unsuccessful because their leader, a being of tall stature, reddish skin and dark clothing, decided not to receive the ancestral humans or the Cassiopeians.

For this reason, soil and surface analyses were performed based on scans and we withdrew from there.

Their beings have advanced structures along their mountains full of vegetation, although they can also be found in the frozen towers.

088 - HYDOR

CODE: N838

These lands have the particularity of a large blood-colored lava volcano, for that reason they were called *"Blood Volcano"* and the most curious thing is that there are creatures that live inside the volcano and go out there during daylight hours.

The *"Hydorians"* are in a technological advance rank A3, and have incredibly resistant structures under the Volcano.

Their morphology is reptilian and they have had conflicts against the Lacertians and Custodians before.
They have come to explore other worlds and our contact was successfully made through our vessel SCB061.
These strongly psychic beings have exchanged technology with Cassiopeians recently.

089 - SADALSUUD

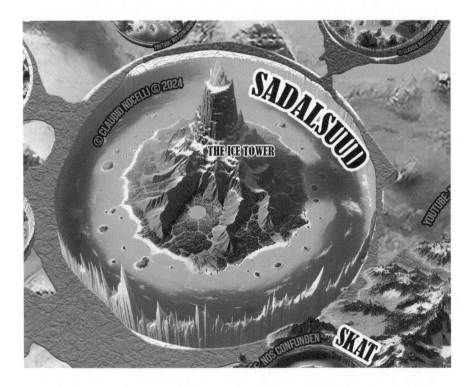

CODE: N839

In the lands called *"The Ice Tower"* there are beings that have built bases towards the top. They are beings that are in advanced development phase of A1 rank and really aggressive with the visitors of their Dome-World.

Our vessel SCB065 was attacked and rescued by two other

vessels. The conflict could have been worse as the native beings there communicate with the Anunnaki. Our craft left that world in time but it cannot be confirmed that possibly the Anunnaki are aware of our travels, this would escalate into a major conflict within the Great Dome that we prefer to avoid.

Sufficient analysis is being done to rule out any attack and to see the extent of the damage from this world's entry.
After this unsuccessful visit, it will also be considered to conduct thorough examinations prior to entry into any future Dome World.

The native beings of this world possess large gray wings and very large dark green eyes.
The top of the great Ice tower is frozen and appears to be empty, but its structures are inside and in the depths.

090 - DARK LANDS

CODE: N840

No life of advanced beings has been found on this world, but several species are in the early stages of development. Possibly they are under the manipulation of another colonizing race.

The race behind this colonization carried out major changes and dangerous toxins that were detected before entering their Dome, therefore, the internal inspection of this world by our vessel SCB078 and SCB079 under reported report "L35-h008" was cancelled.

REPORT L35-h008

Varied environment with wooded areas but with too much fog and thick clouds that make it difficult to see. Its study detailed below was carried out by scanners and radars from the temporary base created on its shores and from our ship. Very diverse climate that changes suddenly reaching absolute darkness.

The creatures found show unusual genetic variation, some species have developed signs of primary social organization.

Unnatural growth patterns, aligned with biological and general environmental modification techniques.

High level of toxins found but future more complex study is needed to break them down and analyze them in depth. The crew will continue to be quarantined until confirmation of any absence of these toxins, in addition the team will carry critical parts in compartments of the vessel back to the initial base.

Any future inspection or additional mission is suspended until the toxins are analyzed and the system is neutralized.

Toxins found on surface:
Neurotoxic - nervous system involvement.
Organophosphorus compound.
Cytotoxic - cell damage Artificially synthesized peptide.
Reproductive - teratogenic compound.

091 - 16 CYGNI

CODE: N842

Creatures in early stage of development. Our ship SCB093 has penetrated this Dome World and has found a large mountain with its respective walls and ridges just behind the large island.

Its creatures are amphibious and are found in various sectors, especially in the swampy area at its core. The report "L37-h192" has been delivered by this ship and Helen has decided not to continue with the analysis of this area and to return the ship to base.

For reasons of secrecy and security the full report cannot be published but something has been found in these lands so Helen has quickly decided to return their ships. Previously we proceeded to the analysis and collection of all possible data on its core.

REPORT L37-h192

Their world is mostly aquatic with fresh water that is also interconnected with salt water by means of fluvial systems and complex hydrological mechanisms built there (too complex for their initial stage of development).

The "Osteopilus" type creatures found have interdigital membranes. Small creatures in the freshwater part that do not reach 16 cm in length are found swimming by their limbs and some possess sturdy hind legs that help them move on land.

The characteristic of their larvae include external gills that can be seen with the naked eye, possibly to be absorbed in later stages of development.
They feed during the dark time of their world, usually on plant matter.

092 - ELENEI

CODE: N843

Creatures found in initial development phase I. Vessel SCB051 has penetrated its Dividing Dome and entered its lands for a better analysis of its lands.

A diverse geography was found with large bodies of fresh water although mostly covered by green and icy mountainous areas. Dense vegetation near its coasts and depths.

REPORT L15-h007

The bodies found are translucent skin that allows the observation of their internal organs in full development. They have larval characteristics with basic internal systems and very limited capacity for movement.

Those found in aqueous environments develop more rapidly, although they seek nutrients in coastal and marshy areas a little further away from their core.
They respond to light and temperature purely by stimuli, the creatures do not have developed reproductive structures and more complex analyses are not yet possible.

These creatures have the possibility of development due to the resources of the environment and their surroundings, except for the intrusion of colonizers.

093 - ALBIREO

CODE: N844

The vessel SCB049 has visited this land and plunged into its depths. It is a very particular land due to its colors with violet tones and dark gray towers.

The creatures here are also in early stage I development. They were found mainly in its core zone near the surface of its waters.

Little vegetation and presence of fresh water although their environment is suitable for the development of the species due to its temperate temperatures.

Its body structure is normal for its species with rudimentary extremities with a length that can reach 20 centimeters.
Tests have been obtained for later analysis in Cassiopeia's central base, although when leaving their world our vessel had serious damage and had to be assisted by the advanced "Iron Blue" crafts.

094 - ALFIRK

CODE: N8152

This world was visited by our vessel SCB024 and has conducted extensive surveys of its interior.
White mountains and vegetation on its shores are found towards the core.

A small, circular, empty island lies at its center where life in early developmental stage II is casually clustered.

095 - ALHENA

CODE: N8168

Dome-world visited by vessel SCB061 but has encountered difficulties on entry as it has barely crossed the dividing Dome received attacks by the natives there or some other advanced race. Other vessels are being sent for exploration and rescue, it is unknown if the crewmen have survived.

The native beings are believed to be in the last stage of initial development III.

096 - ALKAID

CODE: N8130

This Dome World is controlled by the Nibirans and our craft had performed a scan before entering but for some reason had not found or confirmed the presence of advanced structures or bases.

Unfortunately we have lost contact with vessel SCB163 and several vessels and ships have also been dispatched to their rescue. We have not yet received any reports in this regard.

097 - ARTEMISA

CODE: N8111

This Dome-World is controlled by the Anunnaki and the beings that inhabit here were genetically modified and do not belong to these lands either.

It is believed then that the native beings of *ARTEMISA* became extinct due to the manipulation of the environment.

Several Anunnaki pyramids can be found in the northern part of this world.

Their dividing dome has not been breached as surely the beings there would be hostile plus there may be Anunnaki leadership bases inside.

098 - BACO

CODE: N8127

The beings of this Dome World are in phase I development. Its main lands are *"The Black Sun's Passage"* and there are tunnels to the depths that were not explored.

The vessel SCB060 scanned the interior of these lands without finding any structures of other races or traces of other races having developed there.

A report was sent before losing contact with the vessel. Rescue ships have been dispatched to locate it in the area, the reason for the sudden disappearance is unknown.

099 - BOL

CÓDIGO: N8134

Within this Dome-World there are native beings in developmental stage III.

Their morphology is serpentiform and they live inside hollows in the middle of a swamp below the snow-capped mountains that are located on the edges near the dividing Dome.

The vessel SCB108 made incursions into these lands and sent a report after the incident suffered by the ship traveling together.

100 - BÓREAS

CODE: N8145

In this Dome-World are found beings in initial development phase III.

The species found here seems to be of the known species "*Canis Crocutus*". Adults weighing between 30 and 50 kilograms, their length reaches 1.8 meters. With dense fur and varied coloration following some patterns.
Its ears end in a pointed tip with gray tones, its head has a very robust structure and its teeth are prepared to tear and grind meat.

DNA sequence Canis Lupus and Crocuta crocuta, 60% similarity. Key genes: MC1R (skin coloration), IGF1 (balanced body size), PAX6 (enhanced night vision), FGF5 (dense and thick coat length).

This species is found in the lands of *"Marrokh"* in the area reaching the coasts where there is denser vegetation. To the north there are mountainous areas and a large volcano where no life is recorded at any stage of development.

101 - CAPH

CODE: N8155

In these lands there is great vegetation and also life found by our vessel SCB032 that has entered through its divider dome.

Life in early development stage II has been found. This species was added to our database after laboratory studies.

Species: Serpenilinux mirabilis
Weight between 15 and 35 kilograms with length from 1 to 1.5 meters.

Feline-like head structure, strong jaws and very sharp teeth. PAX6 gene (night vision) FTO gene (coat structure and density).

They are found in the coastal and swampy areas of CAPH, as well as in the central island that comprises the core of this World. They move both along the coast and in the water and their speed is astonishing.

102 - CASTOR

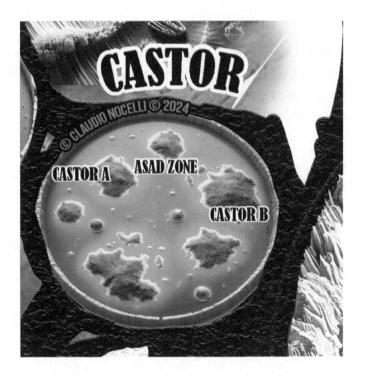

CÓDIGO: N8167

World-Dome divided into several islands and a large ocean that bathes a large percentage of its interior. The islands are divided into *CASTOR A, CASTOR B and ASAD ZONE*. Creatures in initial development phase I.

Our vessel SCB070 was able to enter this world to conduct in-depth studies of its lands, reaching ASAD Zone. Soil samples were taken and the laboratory study of its waters was deepened.

The hydrological sampling resulted in the identification of nanoparticles such as Titanium and Silver. No microplastics were detected. Cyanotoxins detected, a full report on microcystins is attached. Mercury and Cadmium were also detected.

As a result, we can confirm that there is significant contamination of the waters in this environment. Therefore, we confirm the presence of other beings in the not-so-distant past. Further investigation will continue.

103 - CIH

CODE: N8146

Dome-World with a large island at its core featuring frozen mountainous structures and past volcanic activity, currently inactive.

Mountainous landscapes that generate a unique biodiversity and a varied ecosystem. Records of creatures in early developmental stage II were scanned.

Possible vestiges of colonizing bases of the past, we will try to reach the interior of its dome to verify it and if so, to carry out

CLAUDIONOCELLI

an exhaustive investigation for later report.

104 - CLITIO

CODE: C4110

Dome-world where there are vast snowy valleys around the dividing Dome.

This Dome has a complex structure to traverse according to what we have been told by species from the surrounding area who have tried to visit it. Although we did not send ships, we have data provided by our radars and scanners that gave us certain data in search of advanced species and the structure of its islands.

Creatures found in early developmental stage III. No

laboratory studies to add.

105 - DÁNAE

CODE: N8121

These lands were not visited by our vessels because we received a report that a Custodial leader might be inside with a complex underground structure of the colonizers.

Their lands are particular because of the purplish glow of their atmosphere under the Dome and the frozen lands.

This generates beautiful landscapes but dangerous for exploration without advanced technology. Creatures were found in early development stage II.

106 - MERCURY

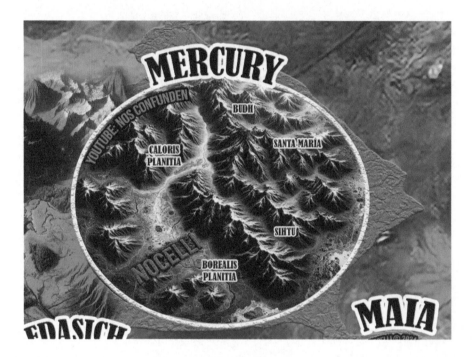

CODE: N8117

In these "*ash lands*" of Mercury, we have not found advanced beings, but structures from a not-so-distant past have been discovered.

The remnants seem to belong to a great empire that was forged here, but the exact time of their disappearance has not been determined, nor the level of technological advancement they had achieved.

These foundations of an ancient culture are located in *Caloris Planitia and Borealis Planitia.*

It is believed that their environment has been modified and manipulated so that today it does not harbor any type of life due to the fact that only arid zones are found. For this reason it has not been possible to send any vessel and penetrating their Dome-Divisor with our "Iron Blue" crafts would be too risky.

107 - DUBHE

CODE: N8139

In this Dome-World there are creatures in initial development stage I.

Its lands are extensive and abundant in vegetation that in turn are bathed by its seas and the great life that exists there of primitive life.

Ships will be sent to obtain more information since only scanning missions were initiated by the periphery.

108 - EDASICH

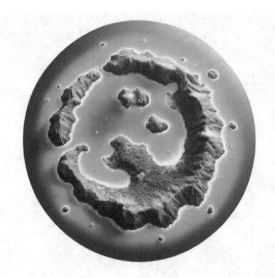

CODE: N8115

In this Dome-World there are creatures in initial development stage II.

Mountainous lands in circular form with crystalline waters, there is great life in the swampy zones that according to information received by beings of neighboring lands are hostile to visit in their Dome-World.

It was avoided to initiate passage through its dome to avoid conflicts with beings in initial phase and not to modify or interrupt its development.

109 - ERRAI

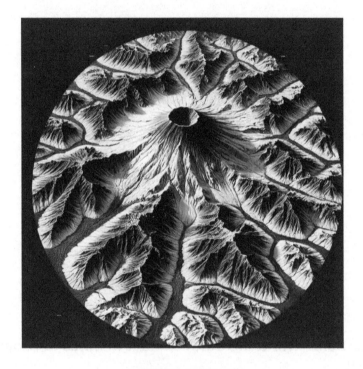

CODE: N8148

In this Dome-World there are creatures in initial development stage I.

Arid and mountainous lands that flow into a large central volcano. Some rivers flow through the southern area but there are not many sea areas there, for that reason no ships have been sent.

It is planned the possibility of sending a ship that crosses its dome by air, but for the moment this world remains in the list of those that will be visited in the last part of the plan and with another type of technology.

110 - ETERNAL

CODE: N851

In this Dome-World there are creatures in initial development stage III.

Vast ocean and lands that remain permanently frozen. Scarce biodiversity that adapts to the extreme climate.

Primitive stage beings resist under these temperatures and mostly reside in deep lands. Navigation appears to be complex due to large ice blocks and frequent storms.

111 - ETHERNAL FIRE

CODE: N8136

In this Dome-World there are creatures in initial development stage I.

Lands rich in vegetation and biological diversity. Its landscapes are diverse, with high mountains and mountains of great altitude under lush forests.

Dense tropical jungles and flowery grasslands.
Its name is due to the glow that appears from the outside as if a great fire were consuming its world from the inside.
Vessels will be sent for in-depth analysis of this Matrix-Cell.

112 - GIANFAR

CODE: N5178

In this Dome-World there are creatures in initial development stage I.

Extensive frozen lands dominate this Matrix-Cell, on its shores primitive life is reported. Imposing coal volcano at its core-center, where its summit and slopes are completely under a large layer of ice covering them.
It is currently reported as active, possibly generating hot springs in its surroundings.

113 - GORGONEA QUARTA

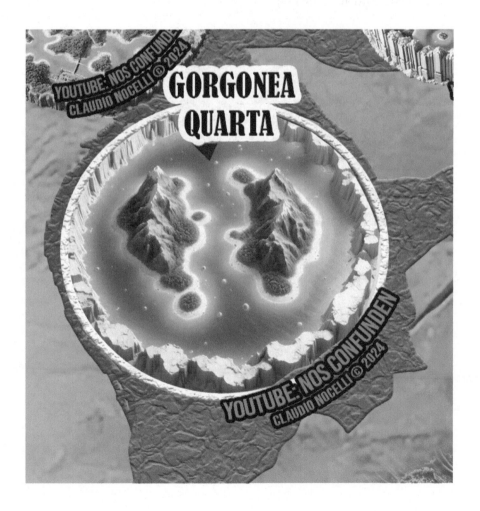

CODE: N849

In this Dome-World there are creatures in initial development stage III.

Life develops on the two large islands facing each other and rich in vegetation, separated by a narrow sea. Although they look similar, both islands have differences based on their ecological characteristics.

114 - GORGONEA TERTIA

CODE: N848

In this Dome-World there are creatures in initial development phase I.

Its lands are very particular and seem to end in the form of leaves, generating great walls towards the white sandy coasts.

It is possible that there is great biodiversity, ships will be sent for research soon.

115 - KURHAH

CODE: N8140

In this Dome-World are found creatures in early development stage II.
Most of the life found occurs in the waters between the vast islands and huge blocks of ice.

We did not find life near its great dividing dome, although the analysis of its waters was not deepened either.

116 - LANDS OF THE SILENCE

CODE: N8166

In this Dome-World there are creatures in initial development stage III. Large expanse of green lands and mountains of ice. Some creatures live under the lands and in swampy areas.

Its main lands are called *"INSIGHT"*. Little sea area that complicate their navigation, attempts will be made to penetrate their Domo-Divisor and analyze their lands by air.

117 - LANDS OF THE STORM

CODE: N8135

In this Dome-World there are creatures in initial development phase I.

In these lands there is a large active volcano in its core, the mountain range near its dome complicates its entry and exit. The climate is humid and large storms are generated continuously.

118 - LANDS OF TIME

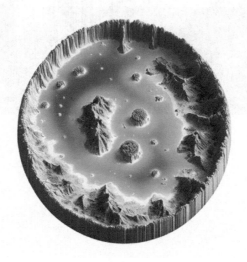

CODE: C486

In this Dome-World there are creatures in initial development phase I.

Its purplish-colored walls create an eye-catching landscape. It is considered that they could have been some artificial creation because they are perfectly closed.

In addition, possible undergound bases were found but no advanced beings have been scanned, further research will be done.

119 - MAIA

CODE: N8118

In this Dome-World there are creatures in initial development stage II.

Lands of extensive vegetation that culminates with a great mountain of silicon that reach great heights. It can be seen from the outside because of its rectangular shape.

120 - MARKAB

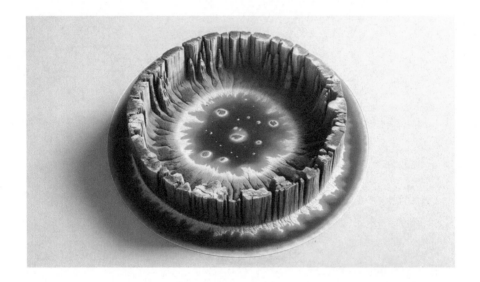

CODE: C483

In this Dome-World there are creatures in initial development stage II. Its walls were imposed in ancient times by colonizers, large undergound bases were found by scans from the outside.

The presence of custodial beings or Anunnaki outside is not ruled out. For the moment the visit to this world is suspended.

121 - MEKBUDA

CODE: N8175

In this Dome-World there are creatures in initial development phase III.

Creatures are found developing in caves between the great Walls that are formed by its high lands. Crystalline lakes are found in the high altitude parts.

122 - MIMAS

CODE: N852

In this Dome-World there are creatures in initial development stage II.

There are large mountains of ice and little vegetation. However, although its climate is complex, there are several forms of primitive life developing towards its coasts and in the great seas.

123 - MUSIC

CODE: N8161

In this Dome-World there are creatures in initial development stage II. Large volcano that occupies large extensions of land.

The sounds it generates simulate a harmonious music due to the movement of the lava in its interior, with respect to its natural vibrations interacting with rock formations and magma, a natural symphony of harmonic sounds are reported from this particular world. No vegetation, life thrives in the ocean.

Possible rich minerals are found in the deep part. This volcano is active. Boats will be sent to the interior soon.

124 - NOVA PERSEI

CODE: N8120

In this Dome-World there are creatures in initial development stage I.

Exceptional biodiversity due to its temperate climate and abundant vegetation. Ideal for life to develop here, easily adaptable.

Diversity of life in initial primitive phase of Grade 1 and possibly 2 is found, but it will be necessary to visit to be able to confirm it.

125 - ORIOS

CODE: C4109

In this Dome-World there are creatures in initial development stage I.

Its creatures are found in caves and in the depths. For this reason and to better study this Circle-Matrix, vessels will be sent to analyze its depth, since according to reports from our scanners it is possible that there is a portal there.

126 - ORO

CODE: N8164

In this Dome-World you can find creatures in initial development stage III.

Due to its extensive vegetation, great biodiversity can be found. Boats will be sent to analyze its interior, especially to delve into the large circular-shaped high mountain at its core.

127 - PERIBEA

CODE: N8112

In this Dome-World there are creatures in initial development stage II.

Large walls of ice near their Dome-Divider enclose these lands, with two well-defined islands. Vessels will be sent to analyze its large central islands of lush vegetation.

128 - PHICARES

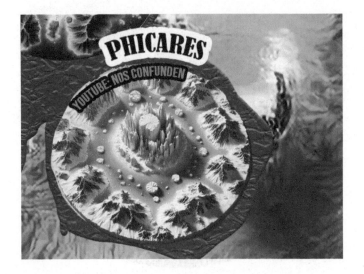

CODE: N8149

In this Dome-World there are creatures in initial development stage III.

A large island of icebergs is found in its core and also around it. Its waters are frozen on its surface.

Vessels will be sent to penetrate its dome and the surface of its waters for in-depth analysis.

129 - POLO

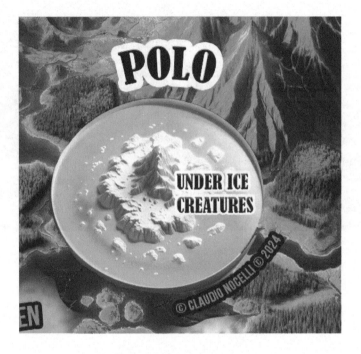

CODE: N8114

In this Dome-World are found creatures in initial development stage II.

Creatures found under the frozen zone of its surface. The temperature inside is totally different.

Our vessel SCB220 has reached its shores and will send a report shortly to update the information.

Its environment is considered to have been modified by colonizers in its remote past. There may be underwater bases by colonizers.

130 - RAI

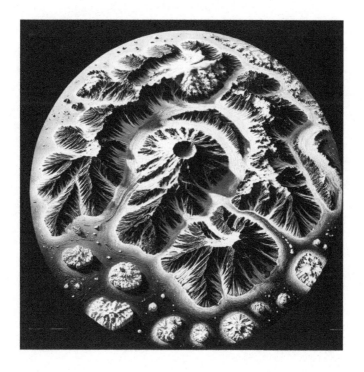

CODE: N8141

In this Dome-World there are creatures in initial development stage I.

Coal lands and inactive volcano in its core. Its waters are gray and its ashes invade its shores. Little life and almost no vegetation, primitive life is found in the ocean.

No ships or vessels have been sent to this world.

131 - RASTABAN

CODE: N8116

In this Dome-World there are creatures in initial development stage II.

Most of the life develops in the part called "*T4*". On the other coasts no primitive living beings have been reported.

The vessel SCB102 has visited this dome, and deepening in the shore part of *T2 and T4*.

132 - ROTANEV II

CODE: N8159

In this Dome-World you will find creatures in initial development stage I.

Several islands dominate this world and most of them end with a mountain with its summit frozen due to the temperature.

Its walls are complex to pass through, so it is considered that colonizers have been here in ancient times.
No current active bases of advanced beings have been recorded. Vessels will be sent for further analysis.

133 - RUCHBAB

CODE: N8154

In this Dome-World you will find creatures in initial development stage I.

Large artificial ice walls, very possibly created by Custodians in the past. Some custodial base in the depths of its waters is not ruled out.
Life is reported to be developing in the core which is under a large dome covered by vegetation.

These lands comprise at least two differentiated domes.

134 - SCHEDAR

CODE: N8151

In this Dome-World you will find creatures in initial development stage I. Primitive life is developing in *"AIDEN" and "MAHAYA" while in "DAO" and "MONAD"* the existence of beings could not be confirmed.

The environment is possibly modified and currently manipulated by the Custodians.

135 - SEGIN

CODE: N8153

In this Dome-World there are creatures in initial development stage III.

Extensive and very high mountain frozen towards its summit exists in this world. The ocean surrounds it and bathes its coasts generating great vegetation and possible great quantity of biodiversity in its surroundings.

In the northern part of this world there is a Portal according to our radars that will be investigated as soon as our ships can enter.

136 - SHERATAN

CODE: N8169

In this Dome-World there are creatures in initial stage of development I.

Its center is dominated by an extensive slope that ends in a conical shape and its fall is similar to silicon. At its core is a crystalline lake surrounded by a particular island that will be investigated when our vessel SCB006 reaches its shores.

137 - SKADE

CODE: N8143

In this Dome-World there are creatures in initial development stage II. Frozen lands where life was found in spite of its harsh climate.

For this reason, it was named the 'Mountains of Eternity.' Our ship SCB010 was dispatched to penetrate its Domo-Divisor and begin an aerial survey of its lands.

138 - SKAT

CODE: N8113

In this Dome-World are creatures in early developmental stage I. Artificial walls by Anunnaki past dominion.

On its *"INN"* lands were found vestiges of ancestral colonizing bases.

These lands are in most of their time in darkness. No ships have been sent.

139 - STEPHENSON

1

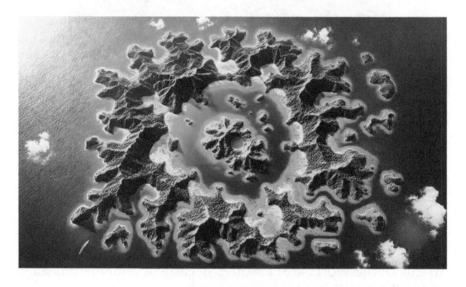

CODE: C4104

In this Dome-World are creatures in early developmental stage I.

Lands dominated by vegetation and white sandy beaches and crystalline sea.

The climate is temperate and life proliferates easily. No ships or vessels have been sent to this world, although a visit is planned soon.

140 - SUALOCIN

CODE: N8160

In this Dome-World are creatures in early developmental stage
I.
Ice Walls that demonstrate a possible colonizing past due to its
way of enclosing this world next to its Dome-Divisor.

At least three well differentiated islands are visualized where
mountains and hills of extensive vegetation are found.
Its climate and environment help the proliferation and
development of primitive life.

141 - TASO

CODE: N8157

In this Dome-World are creatures in early developmental stage I.

Large central island surrounded by natural walls of frozen mountains. In its center there is primitive life in full development.

Our vessel SCB201 has visited this world and has reported in report L39-h609 that several toxins are found in its environment.

Concern about abundant sulfur dioxide and suspended particulates.

Formaldehyde is reported in the southern part of the core. For these reasons, the vessel was requested to return as soon as possible to the central base.

142 - THUBAN

CODE: N8119

In this Dome-World are creatures in early developmental stage I.

Lands that were taken over by Anunnaki in their past, vestiges and possible present active bases were recorded.

No ships will be sent until we can rule out that there are no colonizing beings inside.
A new exploration with radars will be carried out.

143 - TSAO FU

CODE: N8150

In this Dome-World you will find creatures in initial development stage III. Lands surrounded by natural frozen mountains.

Rivers, lakes and seas are found in a large percentage, therefore, their navigation seems to be possible.

No bases of current or past advanced beings were registered. The possibility of sending a vessel is being analyzed.

144 - U SAGITTAE

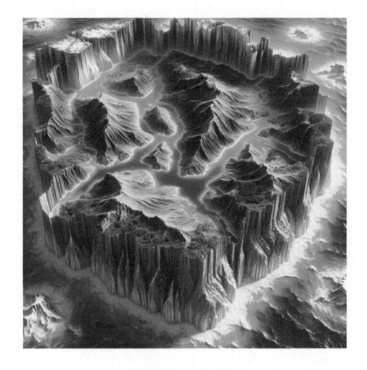

CODE: N8122

In this Dome-World there are creatures in initial development stage I. Small lands dominated by high mountainous and vegetation-rich uplands.

There is a wide variety of plant life and life in development.

The entrance to this world is difficult due to its altitude, for that reason it would be necessary to enter via air first and to be able to scan its lands from the interior. For the time being, no ships or "Iron Blues" crafts will be sent.

145 - WASP

CODE: N8163

In this Dome-World there are creatures in initial development stage III.

Temperate temperature and ample vegetation, gives rise to a proliferation of primitive life.

There are creatures that could be currently in an advanced

stage but just beginning, for this reason we are waiting for one of our vessels to penetrate their dome-divider before confirming it in our database.

146 - WISE

CODE: N5177

In this Dome-World there are creatures in early developmental stage II.

The ecosystem seems to have remained intact for a long time, it is possible that the colonizers have not manipulated this dome, at least, for a long time.
No advanced bases or vestiges of them are also superficially recorded.

147 - SOUND

CODE: N8156

In this Dome-World we have received very strange sounds from its core.

The central part according to our scans is a large energy source under a large dark sphere. Its lands are differentiated from the rest by large mountains of black lands and coal.

No ships have been sent into the interior of this world yet.

148 - CRUX

CODE: C488

In this Dome-World there are beings in initial development stage II.
Their beings are reptilian and live in the different islands with great vegetation and swampy zones.

They were named *"Crossbreeding"* because they have great diversity in their genetics, possibly modified by colonizers in their past.
Their environment is also not free of toxins brought from outside this world.

149 - FROZEN LANDS

CODE: C489

Vessel SCB059 has penetrated this particular Dome-World and has found several creatures in early stage II and III development.

An ancient *"Monolith"* type structure has been reported that could not be deciphered to which past civilization it may have belonged, possibly to native beings that had developed there long ago and for some reason have disappeared.

150 - DAMASÉN

CODE: N845

The *"Damesites"* were thought to be extinct because of past wars with the Custodial colonizers, but after our ships penetrated their dome-membrane we can confirm that they resisted and their race advanced technologically.

Their rank is today in A2 and they have had to retreat in their development but they are still standing.

They have structures within the mountains that are very sophisticated and have made contact with the Cassiopeians in a cordial and mutually helpful manner.

They are spiritually advanced beings of great importance with respect to their scale of beings within this Great Dome who believe fervently in the struggle against the oppressors and colonizers and for the freedom of humanity.

REPORT L44-h302

Assessment was carried out by our two vessels SCB032 and SCB006 to confirm the presence of life forms and the overall current state of the creatures and environment.

Large rocks and mountains of dark brown color due to the sediments of their soil.

Their beings were found living in natural shelters with advanced modifications in the form of dark domes with yellow artificial light.

Sparse vegetation, mosses and lichens that adapted to moisture deficit and extreme arid conditions due to explosions during the past war that wiped out all vegetation.

They possess a complex system that is slowly trying to modify the climate with the help of technology and the environment to generate a restart of their environment and natural regeneration.
The Cassiopeians were in charge of providing them with the information to develop the necessary machinery to carry out their central plan to repopulate their lands.

The Damesites are long-lived in their lands under their own

time within their Dome-World, of humanoid morphology and of average height 1.8 and 1.9 meters.

Due to their spiritual development, they use healing and internal communication techniques that have made them survive their near extinction after the war with the Custodians for the power of their lands.

Their beings have given a report on that war and have confirmed that those who saved their species were the Anunnaki beings as the Custodians had left their lands annihilated and few living beings were left standing.

The Anunnaki helped to recover and then left the area. It is possible that the Anunnaki intention was to return later to benefit from their lands or from their advancement made over long periods.

151 - ATIK

CODE: N847

Creatures within this ATIK Dome-World in development phase III.

Although they are not advanced they have structures all over the outer part of the great central mountain and north of its core.

This world was crossed by the vessel SCB014 but it was not easy and required great efforts and time that was not taken into account since this Dome has double Dome.

The second Dome divides the inner-outer part and then has another Dome that divides the core part just behind the mountains.

Its buildings are generally cylindrical and multi-story towers that rise towards the heights.

152 - R LYRAE

CODE: C4105

In these lands no advanced beings have been registered in activity, possible extinction by colonizers who have modified their environment.

High environmental contamination and toxins have been found in its interior. A request was activated to initiate interior exploration by our vessel SCB027, we are waiting for reports to be added to the database.

According to previous scans, an area of extensive mountain ranges with lush vegetation and possible abundance of life in early stages of development is reported.

153 - XY LYRAE

CODE: C4106

In this Dome-World we find no active life and a great deal of contamination probably by the former colonizers, no exploration has been initiated within its walls.

154 - MERU

CODE: C4107

It was believed that the natives of these lands had been annihilated by their custodial colonizers but according to the last update from our ship sent to that Dome World called *"MERU"*, we were able to verify that there is advanced life in the central zone towards its core.

Its lands are centered on its great silicon mountain and its biodiversity towards the coasts.

Its advanced beings are winged, we have not made direct contact but our vessel SCB177 penetrated its walls recently and has not sent updates so far to add it to our database.

155 - POLIBOTES

CODE: C4108

Custodian colonizers have taken over your lands and formed large underground bases reaching into the core of this dome-world in conjunction beneath your great oceans. Anunnaki leaders have also developed some of their bases here and it is used as a great laboratory for experimentation.

None of our ships have been sent inside these great walls because of the danger of encountering parasitic leaders inside.

There is an icy area with high mountains that can be seen even over its walls.

156 - HELVETIOS

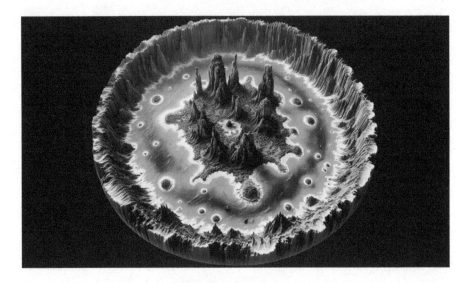

CODE: C484

The native beings here were extinguished by intrusion of the Custodial parasites.

Their Dome-World has been traversed by our craft SCB192 and SCB202 although it was a rather complex mission as several Custodial bases were encountered which from our scans from outside had not been sighted.

By this way the ships were removed in time before any conflict or suspicion of the beings that live there today. Winged creatures of initial development II were also found.

157 - ENIF

CODE: C485

Helen M. has visited these lands in a vessel and confirmed that there are no custodial bases as well as no ancestral human colony as was believed according to information obtained from a strange vessel.

"The Remnant" is the most important area of this Dome-World so close to the Great Barrier-Membrane.

No ships have been sent there again due to its past scanning and because penetrating its Domo-Divisor was very complex. We had significant difficulties in the past due to pressure shifts and changing environments.

VELTO and APON are its opposing lands, located in the eastern part towards its walls.

158 - POLUX

CODE: N8165

In the lands called *"Yang"* coexist the *"Poluxians"*, advanced beings with technology development in the A3 range, together with creatures of colossal sizes.

The Poluxians had in ancient times internal battles and great wars against beings coming from outside the Great Dome, this Dome is called "Dome of Sheol" and the beings have arrived from the outer Dome-World *"ENDOR"*.

These past conflicts, modifications in their environment and genetics changed their morphology as well as their environment.

Today these beings live in the coastal part of "Yang" and also in its seas.

Regarding the ENDOR beings (of fish-humanoid morphology) they are very technologically advanced since they developed very early and today, according to information that could be gathered, they have also taken lands of the South of their Dome called *TANAKH*.

Anyway, due to their constant conflicts and wars, their technological development has been affected in recent times, being in the same range of the Poluxians of A3 according to recent studies.

159 - ARIETIS

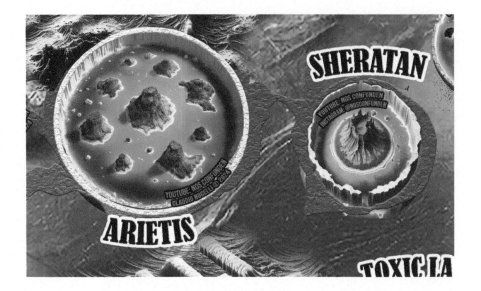

CODE: N8170

During the colonization of the Custodians and the creation of their ice walls, the native beings *"Arietis"* rebelled against them, and their end was tragic since during the war and seeing their impossibility to win, some tried to escape but failed because of the great walls created during the advance and penetration of their Dome-World.

It is unknown if any being born of these ancient lands has been able to survive, but they are considered extinct.

Their morphology was insectoid and we do not know the technological advance they had reached, but it is estimated that they had not yet reached the rank of A2. No vessel has been sent since it is considered that there could be custodial bases in their seas.

160 - BRAHMA

CODE: N8173

The beings of this Dome-World are the *"Brahamites"*, spiritually advanced beings of A2 technological development.

They had contact with the past humanity during the first times since they are very ancient beings as well as great explorers.

Their conflicts with colonizers seem to be in the past although they were close to extinction due to the modification of their environment and Anunnaki-Custodial experiments in their homelands.

The vessel SCB201 has visited these lands and the humanoids there have cooperated with information and technology exchange, a report has been sent to our central base of operations.

REPORT L08-h941

The Brahamites have confirmed that they made past contact with the First Humanity, as well as have brought us spiritual knowledge as in the remote past, always seeking spiritual balance and thus expanding it to other worlds.

They know the past human history and its infinite spiritual potential, they consider us "sleeping masters". They have been consulted about the teachings and application in the present, also about past humanity to add to our database.

The Brahamites have been informed of our desire to understand this Dome and the surrounding Domes and establish the harmony sought without colonization or conflict between races.

The natives live in advanced and harmonious spiritual communities. The "sacred" mountains they call as different ways of breathing, for that reason they always look for places on the tops of the mountainous areas.

They also possess crystalline water of which they take to their community by complex systems, there is not in this dome a great quantity of water to consider for that reason it is rationalized and used with advanced systems so that it is not a shortage.

161 - ALCOR

CODE: N8137

Our vessel SCB018 has penetrated its dividing Dome and has entered these great lands of Alcor. Green is predominant, although ice also appears in its great mountains and volcanoes.

REPORT "L59-h305"

We have encountered *"Lacertian"* beings that have taken over these lands in their entirety.

The original beings continue their development without inconvenience but genetic manipulation has been found in them according to preliminary studies on biology and these supposed Lacertian implications.

Unusual anatomical structures and physiological capacities developed with unexplained jumps have been found in these beings. Confirming that their DNA has been altered.

The Lacertians act as overseers trying to prevent the native beings from having direct relations or communication with our craft.

A base call has been requested to explain the situation and the sending of this report before initiating further actions that could endanger the creatures in the initial phase.

Alteration in the ecological balance and general environment has also been found, a more complex study is needed to determine the damage to the original habitat.

Native beings today possess important adaptive advantages and for that reason their development will proceed more rapidly. Lacertian leaders will be contacted to add important information to this report.

162 - MIZAR

CODE: N8138

The *"Lacertian"* beings have taken over these lands but the native beings there continue to live in harmony. Although it is believed that they have suffered certain genetic modifications which are under investigation.

Our vessel SCB202 has visited these lands although the Lacertians there did not agree. For this reason, some tension has been generated between the Cassiopeians of the ship and the Lacertians who were living there.

The native beings are in initial development stage III. Several reports were sent in this regard and the environment and the mentioned beings are still being studied for some genetic modification found.

The Lacertians are also aware of this, for this reason reinforcements of SCB201 and SCB073 ships were sent, then they left the Domo-World when they retreated so that a major conflict would not start.

163 - LANDS OF THE FORGOTTEN HUMANS

CODE: N8142

These lands have something very particular: a portal has been found in our *lands of origin* that leads to areas close to this Dome World. Therefore, it is known that the Custodians manipulated human vessels to reach these shores and establish a human colony there.

In my book *"The Navigator Who Reached the Sky-Projecting Walls"* we speak of Birsha and Declan, the siblings who were manipulated by a custodial voice through their radio from their craft, and "locked" in these lands.

No craft has been sent to this area, the current status of the human colony there is unknown, but it is confirmed to have existed, at least in a remote time.

164 - ALDULFIN

CODE: N8162

In this Dome-World life is developing at the initial developmental stage III. Although their beings are advancing, they are not yet capable of making contact because it would not be beneficial to interfere with their development.

No advanced structures or traces of colonizing races have been recorded on these grounds.

A more detailed report will be conducted once the thorough study of the area and the species developing here begins.

165 - TOXIC LANDS

CODE: N8172

Lands where their environment was totally polluted and modified in ancient times and where life inside is totally ruled out.
No vessels have been sent and no scanning has yet been carried out.

166 - BABCOCK

CODE: N8126

Yesh, Ka, Mid-RA and AYIN, their main lands. This extensive Dome-World called BABCOCK was also taken over long ago by the Lacertians (reptilians).

For that reason no ships have been sent after the conflicts with them on the different worlds, but, scans were made from outside and information taken from other surrounding lands.

It is believed that the native beings that live there and coexist with them (lacertians) also suffered genetic and environmental modifications.

167 - HYDRA

CODE: N8128

These lands were also taken by the Lacertians recently. It has the particularity of a large circular hill where investigations were initiated to determine what lies underneath.

The Lacertians there contacted our vessel and then with their peers in their bases, requested the immediate withdrawal of our vessel SCB153.
Which once completed the studies and data collection of their land has crossed again its Domo-Divisor to the outside.

168 - ERIS

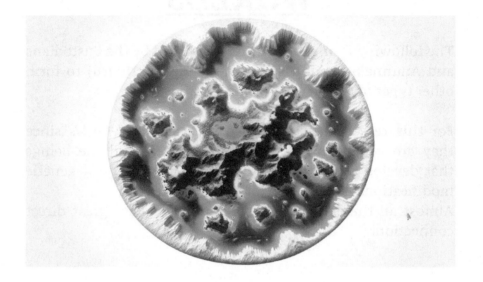

CODE: N8129

In *ERIS* there are Lacertians who have also taken over these lands, therefore, it was avoided to send ships, first it was considered that our ship SCB153 could again enter this Domo-Divisor but it was avoided to avoid major conflicts with the beings who have colonized there.

Scans were performed with our advanced technology systems of Cassiopeia in order to have a better understanding of this Dome-World.

NUCLEUS-DOME *WORLDS*

The following Dome-Worlds were modified by the Custodians and Anunnaki (some also by the beings of Nibiru) to form other types of life than the original-native.

For this reason they are called *Nucleus-Dome Worlds* since they are generally bases of the colonizers and the beings that develop there are hybrids or beings with great genetic modifications that develop for their own benefit.
Almost all these 10 worlds correspond or have great direct connection.

169 - NUCLEUS 270

CODE: C426

Hybrid beings (reptiles) develop in this Dome-World and are in development phase II, under constant Custodial monitoring.

Many internal wars in an early stage of development caused great destruction in this world. Later genetic modifications were also carried out by the colonizers, as well as modifications to their environment to enhance their development.

170 - NUCLEUS 272

CODE: N850

Hybrid beings are developing in this Dome-World (their morphology is unknown) and are in development phase II with constant Custodial monitoring.

Due to the environment of their lands, it is believed that there is a lot of life under the waters and that possibly from there the development towards the coasts and surrounding islands began.

There are no significant conflicts to consider at the moment, but it is likely that the Custodians will initiate internal wars in this world as the beings continue to develop.

171 - NUCLEUS 274

CODE: N8171

Hybrid beings develop in this Dome-World and are in development phase I with constant Custodial monitoring.

Hybrid beings are developing beneath the great volcano that has ice at its peak. These beings have a reptilian morphology but are developing in climates entirely different from where such beings typically survive. For this reason, it is considered a significant genetic modification caused by the colonizers.

172 - NUCLEUS 276

CODE: N8158

Lands monitored by the Nibirans, their beings are arachnids that are in development stage II.

The beings in a primitive phase live in the heights of two great mountains. There are periods of extreme cold that complicate their development. Nonetheless, it is believed that this environmental modification was carried out by the Nibirans themselves.

173 - NUCLEUS 280

CODE: N8174

Extinct beings, the developmental stage of the beings here suffered an extreme change in their environment by custodial manipulation and for some reason they decided to end life or perhaps it was an experiment that ended in the worst way. Today there are no reports of beings living there.

174 - NUCLEUS 282

CODE: N8147

Lands monitored by the Nibirans, their beings are arachnids that are in development stage III.

The primitive beings of this region live along the coasts that flow through vast lands. At its core lies a great mountain where another kind of life is also developing (another possible experiment by the colonizers).

175 - NUCLEUS 284

CODE: N8131

Hybrid beings are developing in this Dome-World and are in development phase III with constant Custodial monitoring.

In this world, there is a significant difference in climate between the connection points of the various regions. The hybrid beings live in the southern part of this world, in areas of abundant vegetation and temperate climates. Crossing the great river marks the beginning of the cold climate area, creating a well-defined distinction.

176 - NUCLEUS 286

CODE: Y563

Lands monitored by the Nibirans, their beings are arachnids that are in development stage III.

Nonetheless, it is believed that recently the colonizers have reset these lands with the possible reestablishment of hybrid beings. The real reason is still unknown.

177 - NUCLEUS 290

CODE: N841

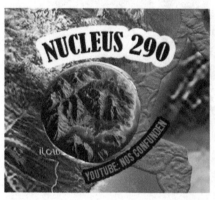

In this Dome-World hybrid beings (reptiles) are developed and are in phase III development with constant Anunnaki monitoring.

This kind of beings is highly developed and has large fortifications on the mountain peaks. No major conflicts have been recorded, but there are leaders in different regions.

It is possible that they have already entered the development of A1 technology.

178 - NUCLEUS 294

CODE: N8144

On this Dome-World hybrid beings are developing and are in advanced A1-range technology with constant Anunnaki monitoring.

Their large communities are centered in the northern part of this world, under a large mountain of cold climates. These beings usually live in the interior of the lands and have created complex ventilation systems in order to create more tunnels to the depths.

THE INDEPENDENT ISLANDS

These lands are not within any dome and are called "Independent Islands" or "Free Lands". Most of them were taken over by different beings who have gone out to explore from within their own Dome-Worlds.

Also many of them are found with advanced bases or vestiges of them since they are or were used for resting or recharging points to other points far away from this Great Dome. There is a great amount of Free Lands, here we name the most important ones.

-*Absolute Zero Crater*
-*Custodian-Real Sector*
-*AOS (Anunnaki Operating System)*
-*Islas Della Punizione*
-*Custodian Tower*
-*Gilgamesh Land*
-*Lands of Endiku*
-*Gran Isla Vergessene*
-*Greys Lands*
-*Land Der Ernüchterung*
-*Lands of Mut*
-*Lands of Atum-Ra*
-*Lands of Ninmah*
-*Lands of Seth*

-Lands of Insectoids
-Northlands
-Osiris
-Resurrection Lands
-Shangri-La

ABOUT THE AUTHOR

Claudio Nocelli

Born in Buenos Aires, Argentina,
Lover of occult stories since I was a child, I followed the skies closely after spending hours reading about UFOs and everything related to extraterrestrials. But something did not fit me in those interstellar travels until the story of the navigator would finally dispel so many doubts, in addition to the ideas of ancient books of mythology and travel that created a possible connection with lands and planets behind the Poles, everything began to have another perspective and sense, especially regarding the human past and the infinite spiritual potential.

Creator of the YouTube Channel: "Nos Confunden" and "Nos

Confundieron" with more than 10,000,000 views

Author of the TERRA-INFINITA Map and following books:

-"The Navigator Who Crossed the Ice Walls: Worlds Beyond the Antarctica"
- "TERRA-INFINITA, Extraterrestrial Worlds and Their Civilizactions: The Story told by the Woman who was Born in the Lands behind the Ice Walls"
- Lands of Mars: 178 Worlds Under the Great Dome
- Lands of Custodians: 178 Worlds Under the Great Dome
- Hidden Lands Beyond the Antarctica: The Continuation of Morris' Journey between Interconnected Planets
- TERRA-INFINITA, THE TRILOGY
- TERRA INFINITA, The Detail of the Worlds and The Theory of the Other Domes
- The Navigator Who Reached the Sky-Projecting Walls
- My Journey to Antarctica: Crossing the First Dome
- The Dome and Outer Space Projection: Year 1728, The Last Reset

TERRA-INFINITA

The journeys of Morris crossing the Antarctic barriers will lead us down paths we never imagined, to the civilizations behind the Ice Walls, the profound ancestral knowledge found there, the story of his daughter Helen, Captain Butler, and Claudio Nocelli's last journey to unknown lands. The 178 Worlds under the Great Dome and the theory of Other Domes that also surround ours make this series a unique and unimaginable journey into what has always been hidden. Welcome to TERRA-INFINITA, these stories will make you question everything you thought you knew until today

- Continents and Dome-Worlds surrounding our "Known Lands"
- Resets (beginning and ending of human cycles) carried out by colonizing beings controlling from the shadows (Custodians and Anunnaki)
- Knowledge about the origin of humanity and its connection to the Celestial Lands
- The real function of the many Pyramids found throughout the Known Lands
- The details of the 178 worlds that integrate this Great Dome
- The Discovery of Other Domes around us
- The knowledge of ancestral humans and the information found in the Great Library
- The importance of the Anakim Giants and other races (such as the Patagones of the South) and their direct connection to the human past
- The Invisible Dome Projector (IDP) that keeps us in ignorance and within the Ice Walls.

The Navigator Who Crossed The Ice Walls: Worlds Beyond The Antarctica

The story of navigator William Morris who, after the Independence War in the United States, decides to investigate with his new vessel the waters surrounding the Antarctic Circle, finding an unknown passage to an open sea. Other lands await him behind, along with another civilization, the story will begin to reveal to the entire group another reality based on the true past and future of the human being. It will finally lead him to the discovery of other worlds behind the Antarctica and most importantly to know himself, a unique journey from which nothing will ever be the same again.

Terra-Infinita, Extraterrestrial Worlds And Their Civilizations: The Story Told By The Woman Who Was Born In The Lands Behind The Ice Walls

The story told by the woman who comes from the lands behind the ice walls, in the "Ancestral Republic", daughter of the navigator William Morris, who will provide information that was hidden from us for a long time about the worlds that are crossing the poles and the secrets of extraterrestrial civilizations. We will also be able to discover the human history before the Last Reset and the continuation of what happened to her father when he returned to our lands. This can change everything.

Hidden Lands Beyond The Antarctica: The Continuation Of Morris' Journey Between Interconnected Planets

Helen Morris, the daughter of the navigator born in the lands behind Antarctica, gives us more details about the continuation of her father William's journey, the Giant-Humans and the hidden petrified trees, the importance of returning to our lands, the contact with other beings coming from other Planet-Domes and the stories and secret information kept in the Great Ancestral Library. Each chapter gives us more clarity about the worlds and civilizations that surround us, this story will immerse us in a unique journey into the human past and future and above all an inner journey into our true human essence.

Terra Infinita, The Detail Of The Worlds And The Theory Of The Other Domes

Welcome to the knowledge of the TERRA-INFINITA in all its dimension, the Great Dome or the Great Barrier-Membrane will break forever to give way to the "Other Domes" that await behind, another new barrier overcome in such a short time.
The Ancestral Humans with Helen as their new leader set out on an unprecedented adventure to blaze unexplored trails in their travels that will open doors that have never been reached before. With the help of Hiurenk's technology they will transport us to other worlds and new horizons, we will learn the details of each one of them from the Great Ancestral Library Database, as well as the new contacts with beings from other Domes that surround us.

My Journey To Antarctica: Crossing The First Dome

A unique journey of no return through the frozen waters of Antarctica and beyond that will provide us with answers that may change the perspective of how we see the world today. The first contact with the ancestral humans and the Anakim giants that live on the other side of the ice barriers and the first invisible dome, the learning of the past that was ripped from us about human history, its cycles, the many resets and a war that seems to have no end against the colonizing parasites.

The Dome And Outer Space Projection: Year 1728 - The Last Reset

In a world where reality is not what it seems, the true nature of the "Invisible Dome Projector" is revealed, an enigmatic structure covering the known continents of this Dome-World, with a simulation of the cosmos designed to shape our thinking. This book explores how, over the generations, the Custodians and the Anunnaki have used advanced technology to not only project a fictionalized version of the universe, but also to manipulate human perception and destiny away from our true purpose and surroundings.

Made in United States
Orlando, FL
25 September 2024

51942672R00241